# The Bonplezi Family

The Adventures of a Haitian Family in North America

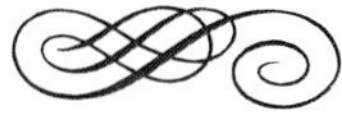



**Maude Heurtelou**
**Educa Vision**

**Educa Vision Inc.,**
2725 NW 19th Street
Pompano Beach, FL 33069
Telephone: 954 968-7433
E-mail: educa@aol.com.
Web: www.educavision.com

The original version of this book was *Lafami Bonplezi.* It has been translated into English by John D. Nickrosz and revised in 2017 by the author. The painting of the cover: "The Road to Success" is an artwork of Dr. Ludner Confident. It is copyrighted by the artist.

Library of Congress Cataloging-in-Publication Data

Heurtelou, Maude
[Lafami Bonplezi. English]
The Bonplezi Family: The Adventures of a Haitian Family in North America / Maude Heurtelou: translated into English by John D. Nickrosz.
p. cm.
ISBN 1-881839-69-9
1. Haitians--Canada--Social life and customs--Fiction. 2. Haitian Americans-- Social life and customs-- Fiction. 3. Haitian American families-- Fiction
I. Nickrosz, John D. II. Title.
PM7854.H39H482513 1996
843--dc21 96-52920
CIP

To

**Dr. Rodrigue Mortel**

A role model for the Haitian Community

## Acknowledgment

The author wishes to express her special thanks to:

**John D. Nickrosz** for the original English translation.

**Dan Connolly**, for his dedication in reviewing the final draft and

**Dr. Ludner Confident** for creating the painting *The Road To Success* for the cover.

## Note from the publisher

John D. Nickrosz, as a translator acts as a go-between to reveal to us the literature of other cultures and languages knowing that quite a lot from the source can never be carried over completely. His translation of Lafami Bonplezi is an achievement because he preserves the simplicity and poignancy of the scenes, keeps the forceful narrative drive, nuances, overtones, and also renders the characters and objects originality... This is a great accomplishment.

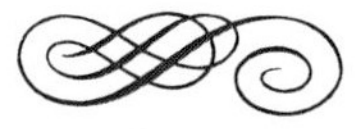

## Before you Begin

The Bonplezi family is an adaptation of a play written for the radio. It is being presented here in printed form because many people who have heard it played have said they would like to be able to read it too. Teachers especially would like to be able to put it in thew hands of their students. Of course, this is not a school book; it is a book about life. The life of Haitians, in all that makes them proud, happy, sad, hopeful, disillusioned, fearful, arrogant and respectful... There are those who like to hear and there are those who like to read about Haiti and Haitians; this book is for everybody.

While Lafami Bonplezi is fiction, it is at the same time a faithful rendering of an aspect of the social reality of Haitians who are living outside their country. The novel depicts the hopes, beliefs, courage and tribulations of our people while at the same time underscoring our simplicity, goodness, pettiness, customs and prejudices. Our reality is depicted in such a way that makes us reflect upon it, laugh, sigh, and shake our heads before we continue to live with a desire to improve.

Lafami Bonplezi is fiction. It presents poor people who are happy and rich people unhappy. It shows us that good and simple people can succeed. It shows us how ours aspirations and our children ones can be fulfilled, even if we are not rich. It reminds us that our children can achieve, wherever they are, even in the country we live in as immigrants. It also shows how we can play the game of life but how sometimes, we are not even in the game of passing and shuffling the cards at all... and end up with nothing in our hand...

They always say Haitians are actors, well; this book is also a glance at the play of our lives...

Lafami Bonplezi also talks about the hope Haitians for Haiti. The people in the book are always talking either bad or good about Haiti... Their umbilical cord is connected to it.

The characters are not real. Let us say they do not really exist but you may know a lot of people who resemble them.

Lafami Bonplezi has appeared originally on audio format as a play about an imaginary Haitian family This is the reason the book presents a dramatic tone that is suitable for radio-theater.. Reading it is one thing and hearing it is another. There are people who prefer the audio version because hearing the actors' voice gives more life to the work story.

This book is the first in a series on the Lafami Bonplezi. As more events continue to occur to the members of the Bonplezi family, we will continue to write them down. We hope this family will entertain you, while you will think about the likelihood of their message.

If, in the course of your reading, you come upon an idea that you do not agree with, keep reading. We want to entertain you even when we disagree! If you want to send us feedback, send them over, we will enjoy them too. They will add fertilizer to our imaginary garden of events. That way, the next book will carry your inspiration as well.

Lafami Bonplezi exists thanks to a lot of coming and going between my good angel and me. It has been published thanks to the endless support and contribution of my husband, Féquière Vilsaint, who is instrumental in my journey of becoming a Creole writer. I have always spoken Creole. Now, I am graduated in writing it! I am not yet an expert but I am doing my best because I love it. I know I have some catching up to do but I will get there one day. For now, my call is to contribute to a corpus of literary material in this language. I remember when as a child I used to get punished in school when caught speaking Creole. Now, I see language as instruments and I want to use them, especially Creole, to sing the beauty of my country, my people and my culture. I have the hope that as more of us discover the beauty of Creole, this language will be more respected.

I would like to mention the names of Yveline Francis Paul and Dr. Harry Borno, who were the first to witness the birth of Lafami Bonplezi. Their encouragement and comments kept me going. They, along with Bervin Bastien, Leonard and Dr. Ludner Confident, Dorothy Borno, Josette, Eunice and Olivia Laborde, Edouard Jean-Pierre, Féquière Vilsaint and Josette Toulmé put time and devotion into recording the audio version. We never really got it in the market but enjoyed every moment we spent recording it. It was a time to reconnect with the past or discover the endless folds of our rich culture. Later, we had the opportunity to air the audio version on WLRN for the Miami and Fort Lauderdale audience. Many Haitians and non-Haitians were delighted to savor that soap-opera. job.

I had great joy writing this work. Every time I read it, I feel a great deal of pleasure and reflect a lot. I cannot describe my feelings when all the members of the Bonplezi family talk at the same time, faster than I can write. Then I start writing furiously, especially when the events get juicy. Those moments remind me of my grandmother Cérès Simonise Pardo, who was a great storyteller... She would laugh so loud if she was still alive... I still think of her as being present, listening, suggesting... and laughing out loud!

There is, however, one person whenever I write, who is always present in my mind, a very special person to me, my good friend and uncle, Marcel Pardo, who taught me to read and write even before I started kindergarten. I shall always be thankful to him, forever. He is my friend for eternity.

Finally, a special thanks to John D. Nickrosz who translated this book in English with a great deal of motivation to respect and maintain the Haitian flavor of the Creole original; Dr. Ludner Confident for creating the painting *The Road To Success* for the cover and Dan Connolly, a teacher at Richard D. Murphy School in Boston, MA who reviewed it and suggested highly appreciated recommendations.

*Maude*

## In The Beginning...

There was a good man who came from the city of Miragoâne. His name was Big Sonson. His real name was Gaston Bonplezi, the grandson of Roro Bontan. He was the town clerk there and had a little business that often took him to Port-au-Prince. Once, on a trip to the capital, he met Miss Marilisi, at the home of Biron Boisson, Justice of the Peace of Bois Verna. After a courtship that was happier than could have been expected, Marilisi and Big Sonson got married one Saturday morning in the church of Saint Anne. Their reception was a big event that lasted the whole day. It was held in a big mansion on the shores of Rivière Froide.

As the bridegroom had prophesied in his fifty-page-long speech, Marilisi's and Big Sonson's future would turn out to be an extraordinary adventure. Of course, nobody at the wedding could have imagined that life was going to be so true to the bridegroom's words.

The wonderful life of the town clerk joined in marriage to that of the mistress of the domestic arts school founded by Marilisi herself, led the couple to engender ten children, eight of whom, Glory be to God, survived. Life made the family witness to all sorts of experiences, yet all the children were given a profession and lofty ideals that few of their neighbors' children received.

The family's life was so very interesting that people from all over would come and go through the neighborhood asking each other. "What's new"... "What's happening at their house?" "Their," you can imagine, always referred to the members of the Bonplezi family.

The best news is that one day, just like any other day, the men and women of the Bonplezi family, started leaving one by one; they were going up there... This was something to be expected, the way the family had been riding high. But, it is the way it all happened that is strange: TiJan, the eldest of the children, who had flunked rhetoric class a couple of times, that is, had failed to get his baccalaureate degree, got an accounting degree in a technical school instead. One day, he took an American Airlines flight like a person moving out of sight and finally disappearing in the traffic. By the time the news reached the neighborhood, by the time the gossip reached the home of Madame Robert at the edge of the crossroads, four more of the children had left!

Looks like an emergency!

It was the crushed ice vendor across Ruelle Jardin who finally gave the last piece of gossip: "Well, they are finally all gone! They left Big Sonson and their mother behind!"

Everyone in the neighborhood knew that the offspring was gone abroad and has left the old folks behind but nobody would talk about it to the old folks. Some neighbors may have found it quite disrespectful that they leave town without saying goodbye, but, the Bonplezis are big shot; they never feel the need to apologize to society. So, everyone continues with their life. No explanation is given.

Those who knew the family well were aware that one of the sons had stayed behind, Gérard, the school teacher.

Since the Bonplezi family was the soul and spirit of the neighborhood, because everybody always wanted to know what was going on at their house, some people continued to wonder and ask about the Bonplezis abroad. They would ask people who came back from up there: "Did you hear anything about the Bonplezis?" "Have you seen any of them?" "What are they doing in the white man's country?" I myself never knew them personally but I made a point of finding out about them.

The interesting thing about this family is the way it resembles so many people we know, so many people you must know too. The story of the Bonplezi family is so interesting, so typically Haitian, that we would love to have a little piece of it to nibble on. The Bonplezis are settled in various parts of the United States and Canada.

I do not know if you have noticed this before, but in every family there is one house where everybody likes to gather from time to time. Well, in the Bonplezi family, it is at the home of Jean, TiJan, for the intimates, where everybody always lands. Even when Big Sonson and ManPlezi come to the United States, it's always at TiJan's they stay, even if only for the first leg of their trip.

TiJan and his wife, Carmen, live in Miami. That's where Paul and Gaston Junior live as well. There are other siblings in New York, Chicago, even as far as California. Solanges, however, is in Montreal. This means there is a lot of traveling back and forth in the family. Are you ready?

Today, in 1992, more than twenty years after TiJan left Haiti, after marrying Carmen (Tika, for the intimates), he is now 48 years old. He has three children...It is very true that time whirls by us like a top loaded with events...

It is TiJan, the oldest, who is responsible for having gotten three fourths of the family over here in the US... He fulfilled his duty towards the family!

But, as the bridegroom had prophesied at his parents' wedding in his memorable long speech, many other surprises would come to pass in the life of their offspring. Life had only begun.

Today, twenty-three years after TiJan's left Haiti, the Bonplezi family is not the same any more. Each one has made their own way. Each one is living their own reality. Some of them have made it big. Some are still behind, living day by day. The offspring has gone through different kinds of events. The history of Haiti has moved through their lives and through their homes.

The Bonplezi family represents all kinds of Haitians, every class, every level, in every sense of the meaning. They are people you want to know about even though you may never have met them. Ladies and gentlemen, here is the BONPLEZI family!

Today is Saturday, around five o'clock in the afternoon. We are at TiJan's house.

# CHAPTER 1

## A Family with Principles

- Jean, how can you be so calm? I don't like it when you sit like that, with your hands on your chin. You are thinking, aren't you? What's the problem? What are you thinking about?

- Carmen, I don't like it when you interrupt me in my thoughts. My head is loaded with things that are worrying me, and I don't always feel like talking!

- You don't have to get angry, *monchè*, I can see that for a few days now your mind has not been with us, I'm worried...

- You have reason to be worried, *machè*. When you are raising three children in the United States, one can say it's a blessing to thank God for if none of them is into drugs or any unconventional situation. But, that's not all... Steve is ready to go to college, we put him on this earth; we have to give him the means to succeed. What's on my mind is my son's future... Such an awfully bright boy!

- The problem is we didn't know enough to put money aside for his college! It isn't like Haiti here. In Haiti, I can remember, one didn't need money...The university was free... but you had to have connections! There is only one thing that's keeping me going about this matter is prayer. I pray every day. We have to find a way to get the money for his college. Through all these years, Saint Jude has kept me going. In New York, whenever I used to ride back and forth in the subway, or go food shopping on foot and have to walk up these five flights of stairs of the old building, you remember, whatever I was doing, Saint Jude never left me. This time, he's going to still be with me!

- Prayer is okay! But I still have to do my part. I can't let this thing keep worrying me. Steve has to go to college... Well, Tika, let's change the subject. No one from the family has called? Can you believe it has been two weeks since one of them has called...!

- TiJan, you know very well that your family rarely telephones us. It doesn't seem like bringing your family over to the United States to live near you is something one should ever do. Now, we have learned our lesson... Everybody I know says the same thing: As soon as they get in, they turn into the whip that beats you! Before they came, remember when you used to call them on the phone, remember, they were all yours. Remember how much they used to say they loved you; I am the best wife you could ever have. Remember? You sent for them, and now, they have their own lives. They have no time for you and me. They had turned their backs on us...

- Sometimes I wonder if, in the family, we still love each other the way we did in Haiti. Wouldn't you say we are rather like enemies? We don't see life the same way; we don't have the same principles. My God, who would have guessed it!

- Now, relatives don't know each other anymore.

- Everybody's forgotten what uncle, aunt, cousin and godmother means! I know our children are Americans, but I want them too to be raised as Haitians. They can babble off in English but I want them to keep their Haitian principles and be able to speak Creole and French too...! By the way, did you get any news from anyone in the family today?...

- No. I just told you nobody has called. I didn't call anybody either. The family is growing apart. Gaston is the only one who keeps in touch with us... So… What are you going to do? Do you want to call him?

knock, knock, knock....

- Do you think it could be Gaston? Tika says aloud to herself. That knocking sounds like him. Gaston, is that you? I was just talking about you. Where have you been?

- I've been around, Tika. I've been thinking a lot about you guys lately, but, I've been very busy. I've had meetings too, you know you have to keep on going...

- Sonson, inquires Tika, what's up in the country now? Nowadays I don't hear anything good about home. It's one thing or the other, when will something good happen in Haiti?

- Hold it, hold it, Tika. Don't be pessimistic. You will see, someday something good will happen. The boil isn't ripe yet. When it is, it will burst open, and when it does, the pus will come out too. A good little country like that cannot go six feet under, *machè*.

- Sonson, come to eat! I just prepared some rice with *djondjon* and goat meat. Just from the stove. It's still hot. I have a little bit of eggplant with crab too, loaded with sauce and hot pepper. Come and eat, brother. Let's all seat and eat together.

-You know, comments TiJan, my wife likes to see all of us together, at the table. It was always her dream to have us all sitting around the table... but some of us want to keep to themselves...

- *Monchè*, I don't believe in that at all. We are still connected to each other, somehow. I understand that you could be frustrated because you brought us all over here and we seem to stay away from you. Maybe you had plans for each one of us but, you know, like is not like that. Everyone makes their own plan but we all know you are the patriarch here, brother.

-Hmmm! Yes, brother!

- *Monchè*, you didn't have to make all the sacrifices you did for us. Working two jobs, working both night and day, sacrificing your wife and your children, leaving Tika alone at home all the time or leaving the children for long hours in a day care so you can make money to send for us. When I think of the hardships you and your wife had to go through up in New York, I feel a great deal of appreciation for you both, but, I have to tell you that the reason I keep in contact with you is not out of gratitude. It is more because I love you and the children very much.

-You're saying too much Gaston. You know TiJan and me we were doing it from the bottom of our heart…

-TiJan, brother, listen. Bringing your family over from Haiti is a duty. It's a duty that anyone with connected love and brain shall fulfil with dedication and generosity. It is not a reason to blackmail anyone. It is not a reason to micromanage anyone. Once you have sent for the bird and it has grown wings, let it fly! The higher it flies, more power to him or to her and more pride to you! So, let's don't waste our time complaining. Let's put our heads together and go on living. We still have a country to build, *monchè*! Even if we are settled on these shores, our umbilical cord is connected to *Haiti Thomas*!

-We know that...

- On the name of Saint Jude! We cannot forget that.

-Oh, Tika, is this huge plate of food for me? Oh, sister! You're giving me too much food! I don't have room for all that. Your food is delicious, sis, but, if I eat all that, I'll fall asleep.

-Ok. I hear you…

-And sis. Oh, sis. Allow me to comment that you're too generous with the oil; you should start cutting down on fat, sis. You know all that fat will come down to heart problems.

- You see, acknowledges Tika with appreciation, that's what I like about you, whenever you come, you give me good advice, Gaston. You know, brother, I don't have time to get the news nor that I read those big intellectual books you read. I don't know what's going on in this big world, but I'm interested in learning. What other good advice do you have for me, Gas?

- *Machè* Tika, your food is delicious, but, next time, please don't give me that much... And remember to cut back in the fat. See how my brother Jean is getting a big belly; it's not good for him. Imagine, a young man like him with a big belly! That doesn't make sense, *machè*.

- Sonson, says Jean as he feels his belly with some embarrassment, when you have a time, talk to Steve for me. Have an uncle to nephew conversation with him. Do that for me, please. You know, he wants to go to college. As for me, whatever he wants, I want. However, you know more about the business of going to college than I do.

Jean gets up to call his son Steve. He wants to take the opportunity of Gaston's visit to engage that conversation.

- Steve, come and talk with your uncle Sonson!

-Wait a minute, interjects Gaston, wait a minute, brother. Not yet. Let's think on it some more between us first. I need to know where you, adults, stand first. Then, I will talk to him. I will talk to him, definitely, and, soon...

Gaston changes the subject while helping himself with a spoonful of eggplant in crabs. Too much delicious food that he cannot resist.

- *Monchè*, I've always admired the way you and Tika have succeeded in getting your three children to talk English, Creole and French. You don't know how close that makes me feel to them. I feel they are Americans, but, at the same time, they are Haitians too. They are what I call the hope of Haiti. Those children, tomorrow, when they become congressmen, or, why not, president of the United States, they will remember and think about the respect their father and their mother had for their homeland and they will treat Haiti with greater respect. They will give the country a real helping hand.

- *Monchè*, I don't tell them what they have to do. They're good natured. They're good children... They've always liked school and they pick good friends, too. I have nothing to reproach them. One thing my wife and I believe in is to teach the children to respect us; for us, part of teaching respect is letting them hear us talk about Haiti with pride, teaching them our language so they are able to speak with the rest of the family in Creole when they go to Haiti. We also want them to identify with the Haitian people and our struggle, even as they perceive themselves as Americans, too. I can't deny it.

- *Monchè* TiJan, the other day, I called Mom in Port-au-Prince. She repeated over and over how happy she and Papa were that Steve had had a long conversation with them on the telephone. I really felt good to hear they had that connection. There are a lot of old people who cannot talk with their grandchildren, man! As you know, many children in Canada speak a different kind of French. Those in the United States speak English. Almost none of them can carry an elaborate conversation with their grandparents. Often the grandparents talk only Creole. That is a shame that our culture is losing that multigenerational oral tradition!

- Sometimes, laments Tika, the grandparents live in the same house as the grandchildren and they cannot understand each other. Some people send to Haiti for their parents to take care of the grandchildren and yet the kids don't even respect them! No, that shouldn't happen because in our country, old people are symbol of utmost respect! In Haiti, older people are always right!

- What do you mean old people are always right? asked Jean.

- It means that our elders always have the last word. Old people have authority, in Haiti, TiJan, remember? That's the way it was since I can remember! We were not even allowed to look at them straight eyes to eyes, no? Remember, for example, how when one of the old folks inadvertently made an inappropriate gastric noise, either burp or… you know what I mean, it was the children that had to say "excuse me!" Nowadays, especially in this country, it seems like old people are nothing at all... Well, at least our children have no trouble talking to Big Sonson and ManPlezi. That, I wouldn't negotiate with them.

- Of course, agreed Gaston. And the grandparents sure are enjoying that.

And he changes the subject.

- Jean, are you aware of what's going on in Florida? A lot of Haitians are arriving here by boat, and some of them are caught even before shore and taken to Guantanamo. Brother, you have to see what's happening! It's pitiful to see our Haitian brothers treated like criminals. Even men cry at the sight of it. I cannot stand to see so much suffering, man. I thought I was beyond the age of crying. I didn't think I would live to see my people going through still greater suffering...

- Oh, Gas, you've been to Guantanamo? ask TiJan.

- Yes. I have been to Guantanamo and I have also been to Krome and to the Dominican Republic. Man, that's hell on earth! Now I know, whomever a Haitian over here thinks, whether he thinks he is a big cheese, the pope or some big shot, in fact, he is nothing at all while his people is living under such subhuman conditions. All Haitians, wherever they are, and, I mean it, all Haitians have a huge bag of collective responsibility to carry around, if not in their heads, at least in their hearts, if not in their hearts, well, in their souls! I've said what I had to say. Yes, all Haitians wherever they may be! We are all responsible!

- What you say is true, brother. If you're not bad off and you tell someone here you are Haitian, they tell you: "It can't be true, I don't believe you; you're not Haitian"...As if they could not imagine Haitians living a decent life! How disrespectful...

Brother, tell me how is Margaret doing?

- She's okay. She's all right.

- Well, when are you going to set the date? inquires Tika.

- What date?

- You know very well, Tika replies, your wedding date. You've been together so long, Gas. She's going to wait forever and not a word is going to come from your mouth!? Whatever you do, she's there alongside you. M*onchè*, you could marry her...

- I will marry her, Tika. I might marry her. You don't have to rush me, sis. I'll let you know....

- All right then. So, from what you're saying, if I interpret well, concludes TiJan, when I call Mom on the phone later tonight, I can give her the news...

- What news?

-That you're marrying Margaret.

-Oo? No way, *monchè*. That is not what I am saying. We are not getting married now. There is no reason to hurry. Margaret is a good woman, of course. I like her, of course, but, I would like to take my time...

Tika tries to make him understand her opinion about that matter. That Gaston doesn't seem to have his feet on reality.

- Brother, why do you have to spoil the woman's future? She's not a child any more. She has a career, she is working at a university, and she has already reached her professional goals in life. What are you waiting for, now? You should do it, *monchè*!

- Tika? Tell me you're not talking seriously...! How am I spoiling Margaret's future? When a man and a woman accept to share their time and energy together, even if they're not married, as long as nobody is forcing the other, there is no abuse, I don't see what I can be doing that's so wrong. I don't see how I can be spoiling her future, Tika! I'm not a liar, I don't make false promises, and I don't pile up bluffs. For now, Margaret is my companion, that's it. I'm not ready to get married, or to have children.

- O, *mezanmi*…!Saint Jude…

-Tika, call Saint Jude if you want, but, I am facing other challenges at this point of my life. I don't know what Margaret may have told you or if she told you anything but, in the meantime, if she has a problem with the life we had, she and I, she is free to move on. She can look for her own challenges too. Let her pursue her own career, learn another profession, do whatever she likes. Be it whatever it may...

(Gaston is perspiring heavily. He feels cornered by that perpetual conversation about his marriage to Margaret whenever he comes. Tika seems not to realize how annoyed Gaston is when someone tries to push him)

... However, Gaston continues, if Margaret plan to success is to get married, then, for now, she is a failure. If marriage is her immediate goal, she needs to break up with me and find someone anxious to get married, even if that person doesn't love her, or doesn't respect her like I do. You know, I am puzzled. I can't understand why, as soon as a woman turns eighteen year old, she is already waiting for a wedding commitment, for someone to be responsible to care for her, pay for her fancies, feed her, give her her dream house, buy her expensive jewelry and pay for shoes of every color in the rainbow. Does it have to be me?

- But, Gaston...

-No, Tika. Don't stop me now. That obsession to get married no matter what must stop. Women have to learn to take care of themselves, then, as an autonomous person, they can partner with the man they love when they are ready to commit. That what I will call gender equality!

Gaston goes on and on. He is really upset. He is really going at it. Tika puts her hand on her mouth as if to say she is sorry she ever started this. TiJan is playing with the handle of his fork, as if looking for a way to change the subject. They were both so happy to see Gaston and thy messed up. And Gaston is not done yet.

- Really, I think woman should invest in their autonomy first. So far, it seems that it is only after women experience disappointment in love that they invest in themselves, go back to school and build a career. The way you talk, Tika, it seems as if marriage is women's sole mission in life. If women only knew, they would first get themselves a profession before they tried to get married. There is nothing extraordinary about men, there is no miracle in them. There is no guarantee they make women's life better. A man is someone who is trying to make his way, just as any other person, just like women. He doesn't carry a happiness kit under his arm...

-Ok Gaston. Tika and I we get it now...

Gaston starts lowering his voice as if, after having gotten so upset, he now calms down by himself. He now speaks softly and that really relieves his hosts.

- *Mezanmi*, a lot of women make that mistake, they shouldn't believe in Santa Claus forever...Anyway, as far I am concerned, for me to be interested in a woman, she has to have a profession. If she is looking for a husband as a post to lean on, she is headed in the wrong direction, she is not going to find me!

-But Margaret has a profession, non?

-Tika, advises TiJan, leave Gaston alone, do you hear me? You are getting him upset. He can't even eat his food. Look at him, he's sputters all over the table. See what you did.

Now it's time to get out of the subject and that what everyone seems to feel.

-Whenever you are ready, Gaston we will too, offers Tika apologetically. I am going to pray Saint Jude for you. He's a good saint, if you are under his protection, your life will be as smooth as velvet...

Then, mumbling in the kitchen she continues.

...I understand Sonson, Margaret is a little too intellectual. She doesn't try hard enough to convince him it is time to marry her. Look how long they have been together, she should have found a way to get pregnant. She's not stupid. She knows very well what to do, she's the one who doesn't want it that marriage....

Gaston overhears and now, he is fuming at Tika.

-You're making my blood boil, exclaims Gaston! I don't want anybody to force me to do anything until I'm ready for it. I love Margaret, I want to have children one day but I do not want to get married now only because some saint is going to put a curse on me or an unexpected pregnancy appears as poison in my life. No, no and no! I want to marry when and if I'm ready. And that is how it's going to happen. Not before. Not under any other type of influence. If somebody doesn't agree, marry the first man who comes along.

The telephone rings, interrupting Gaston.

Ring....ring....ring.

TiJan picks up.

- Hello. Yes. Jean Bonplaisir speaking. What? How did that happen? Where is he now? What? Seriously wounded?... At St. Joseph's hospital...? Emergency Room...? Oh, my God! ...We're on our way...!

# CHAPTER 2

## Queen Sandra

Steve, TiJan's and Tika's son, was involved in an accident! He was with a friend his age from the neighborhood, a white kid who doesn't have his head on his shoulders. He took his father's car and drove it without even having a driver's license. He was just learning to drive! You know how kids behave when they are just learning to drive. He went through a red light! He came out with minor injuries. Steve is in serious condition. The car is completely demolished.

Steve got hurt badly in back of his neck. He seems to have a broken leg too. It was the police station that called TiJan's house to inform the family. On the spot, TiJan, Tika and Gaston take off for the hospital with both fear and faith.

Gaston calls Paul, one of his younger brothers who is a doctor. He hopes Paul can be a better support to the family. TiJan and Tika are terrified...When they arrive at the hospital, TiJan is shaking, unwilling to imagine that his only son's life is in danger. Tika, disconsolate, is singing a church hymn to Saint Jude. She feels like passing out. Gaston cannot stand seeing what is going on. After inquiring about the gravity of his nephew's condition, he leaves, tears in his eyes. He cannot take it. Paul better arrive soon to take over his spot....

The family is so emotional around Steve, the hospital staff suggests that they should leave Steve alone in the room and step outside, except for Paul. Paul, as an uncle and a physician in that hospital, is allowed to stay by Steve's side.

Sandra, Paul's wife, also rushes to the hospital when she hears the news. As I am relating to you now, Tika, TiJan and Sandra cannot keep still... Paul is explaining the situation to them. They are now in the corridor of the hospital.

- Oh, Paul, says Tika, Steve's accident brought us together tonight! Thank you for being here with us now. Tell me, brother, will my son be all right? Paul, please don't tell me he will be disfigured1!

- I spoke with the doctor in charge, Tika, they say that in a week he is going to be on his feet. You won't even remember how bad he looks now. He is going to be up and running in no time. Don't worry, do you hear. He'll have a few small scars in the coming weeks, that's all. He will be all right. I am telling you that. The scars won't be anything at all.

- Paul, asks TiJan apprehensively, is he going to be able to study? Will he be able to learn? Didn't he get hurt in the head? Can that affect his intelligence? He is so smart, Paul, I always dream to see him becoming a man. If something happens to him, I might as well die! Look, he's now getting ready to go to college. His dream is taking all we have to send him to Harvard. That's where he's been accepted. That's where he wants to go, all the way up there in Massachusetts.

- So, laughs Sandra, ironically, he is going to become a doctor or something like that! Just like that, you think!?

- Whatever he wants, Tika replies. It's up to him. I don't care what the cost will be. As for now, I only want to see my son whole, without any missing parts. In the name of Saint Jude...

- Well, where was Saint Jude when the accident happened? He is the patron who never let you down...

- He was there, Sandra. He never leaves me and my household. He was there. You see, Steve didn't die. He was there to save his life... I will continue to invoke him, Sandra. I believe in him... I am going to continue to call on him... I will... I will. Thank you, Sandra, thanks a lot, I am going to call on him for you too. I'll pray to him so that you will never live for the day you have to cry over a child, do you hear!

- Both of you, says Paul consolingly, Jean and Tika, you have had an emotional shock. Go sit down outside. Let me, as a doctor, stay inside. I'll stay by Steve's side as much as needed. Go have a breath of fresh air outside, in the hospital yard. Let me talk with the surgeon. Leave everything to me, do you hear? Steve is like my son. I feel bad for him too, but I know he is not in serious danger. You can calm down now...

Changing his mind, Paul suggest:

- Actually, why don't you two go home instead... I'll call you when Steve gets out of the operating room... Okay... Let him sleep. They just medicated him, he needs some sleep. Sandra, darling, go with them. Go in their car and keep Tika company. TiJan will drive you home afterwards. I have to see a colleague here anyway. Stay with Tika at her house for a while, speak with her, comfort her. You're a mother, you can understand her grief.

Paul's empathy for Steve bothers Sandra, naturally jealous.

- Paul, I can understand why you would want to stay with Steve, but, you don't have to say he is like a son to you. He is not your son! Besides, you have three beautiful and intelligent little daughters!... You don't need a son. Why don't you ask Dr. Maglio to take me home instead of your brother. You know the seats of those Japanese cars give me a backache. That is not what you had told me...

- Sandra, this is not the moment for that... will you try to understand. Do that for me. I'll give you a reward later on, ok, darling?

So Paul seems to always be bribing Sandra.

-Sandra, agrees TiJan, if you're not comfortable in our car, you can wait for Dr. Maglio. You know you don't have to worry about us. We will be fine.

- Okay, then, I'll wait for Dr. Maglio.

- Thank you for coming, adds Tika. Sandra, thanks for coming, thanks for everything. Give those beautiful and intelligent little girls a kiss for me. I love them a lot!

- Sandra, insists Paul, I want you to go with TiJan, I won't ask John Maglio to drive you home. He is a colleague, he has no obligation to drive you. That's all I have to say. Go with TiJan. Go ahead and see you later!

TiJan, Tika and Sandra start walking out together. But Sandra stops abruptly. She doesn't like the idea of riding in such a small –and cheap- car. Paul, thinking she is gone, settles down in a chair in the conference room close to where Steve is resting and grabs a telephone to call Gaston.

Ring....ring....ring.

- Sonson, it's Paul. Where did you go? You were just here and you disappeared.

- I am home, brother. I stayed at the hospital for a while but I had to leave. I just couldn't face the possibility of Steve's death. Imagine, Tika and TiJan were just talking to me about Steve. They had just finished asking me to talk to him about his plans to go to Harvard and look what happened! *Monchè*, I really feel bad, it hurts me a lot to think that Steve is hurt in that accident. I don't know how to handle my pain and theirs. I'm just not good in those situations. It's as if their clock had stopped running. Besides, I can't stand to see blood.

- Don't worry, brother. You called me and I came to replace you. I am still at the hospital, keeping an eye on Steve. Between you and me, he could have been killed if the impact was greater. You know, it really hurts me too. However, at least, I know he will make it. He isn't going to die at all! You know, I really love this child!... I regret that with my long hour shift and family responsibility, I don't have enough time to advise him more. I look upon him as my own son. You know, I always wanted to have a son...

Meanwhile Sandra who hasn't left, was standing not too far from Paul who had no idea she was spying on him as she always do. She is always worried of the possibility that Paul could have another woman in his life, ready to grab him from her. For that reason, she always listens in on his telephone conversations. I don't need to tell you how furious she became when she hears him saying he would have liked to have a son.

Such confession to Gaston ripped Sandra's heart apart. Without thinking, she instinctively rushes upon her husband, abruptly interrupting his conversation. He is caught. He only had enough time to tell Gaston that he urgently has to hang up, he has to go. Now he listens to Sandra as she rushes at him.

- Paul, aren't my three beautiful and intelligent little daughters enough for you? Beautiful children with beautiful hair and a beautiful skin color too, isn't that enough for you? How can you admire other people's children, people who churn water to make butter, who have to wear patches on their clothes in order to try to look good, little people of no social value... These are the people you like? Paul, shame on you! Is that what you do to me, me, to me Sandra? You crush my children under your feet?

- Sandra, I want you to be quiet, now! First of all, you are not to talk to me like that in the hospital, and secondly, don't trash my family...

- What family! Tst...! People who live on Martin Luther King Street? We can't even visit them because they live in such dangerous neighborhood!

- Sandra, I order you to shut up right now! You are waking Steve up. You're making a scene in the hospital. Can't you see people are looking at us? Have a little decency.

- You are the one who is being indecent. You have the nerve to insult our children. Think of it, we raised them as little princesses. They play the piano, and the violin. They dance, they perform, they do calisthenics and they paint and you have the nerve not to appreciate them!

- Sandra, it's not a question of not appreciating our children. I love them, I adore them. I was simply telling Gaston that I love Steve. Don't I have the right to love my nephew? Don't I have a right to feel and be free with me feelings? God, you are hard to get along with!

- You have the nerve! Me, hard to get along with! You are the one who grabbed the phone in my absence. In the presence of your so-called nephew, you started proclaiming to anyone at hearing distance that you always wanted a son. What a coward you are to betray your family for this nobody?

- Sandra, Steve is not anybody! And, you know, you are upsetting me...If Steve wakes up and hears you I will never forgive you.

From his bed, Steve moves, trying to change his position. He opens his eyes and looks all around. He is drowsy from the medication they gave him. Paul bends over him with genuine affection. Sandra follows him in Steve's room. Steve looks at Paul and Sandra, he doesn't recognize them exactly but begins to speak.

- Dad, dad, what is happening to me?...I am scared. I feel strange.. What happened? I'm afraid...

- What do you feel, Steve? questions Paul. Talk to me...

-I am scared Dad... Where is Mom?...

-Paul, protests Sandra, boiling of jealousy. Tell him you're not his father at least!

Paul ignores her and continues to focus on Steve.
- ... Am I going to die, dad? ...

-No, Steve. You will be just fine. You are going to the operating room and everything will be all right.

- Aunt Sandra, where is Mom? I need Mom. Where is Mom? I need to talk with Mom.

- Steve, whispers Paul reassuringly, relax. Mom and Dad are coming... I am your uncle Paul and I am here with you. Everything will be all right... Relax.... Hold my hand if you want... I am here with you... Close your eyes and relax...

- Aunt Sandra, I feel sick...headache. Help me please...big headache...

- Don't worry, Sandra tell him coldly, everything will be all right.

- Would you pray for me, Aunt Sandra?... Where is Mom?...

- I don't pray to Saint Jude. I don't pray...,Sandra tells him.

- What happened to me?

- It happened that you are a bad boy, Sandra adds, reproaching.

- What? Sandra, please step outside! Paul tells her, Go call Carmen and TiJan. Tell them Steve is awake.

- Why don't you call them yourself?

- All right, honey. I will.

Ring...ring...ring

- Jean, Steve has just awoken. Sandra and I are with him now. He is asking for Carmen. You two can come down, come right away before he goes into the operating room.

While the couple is on its way back to the hospital to see Steve before he goes into surgery, Paul steps outside. He steps out, expecting to welcome them, leaving Sandra behind. He cannot stand Sandra's attitude, he finds her heartless. Meanwhile Sandra decides to stay in the room alone with Steve. And she engages a conversation with Steve, although he is in excruciating pain.

- Anyway, what you did is very bad, Steve. If you were my son, I would punish you, I would give you a real whipping, you wouldn't have a fanny left to sit on. I would have skinned you alive.

- I didn't do it on purpose. I wasn't the one driving...

- I know, but what you did was very wrong. You choose the wrong type of friends. That's how kids go bad! You are a good for nothing...

TiJan and Carmen arrive. But they have already taken Steve to the operating room. With tears in her eyes, Tika whispers: "I love you Steve, you are my everything1" She raises her two arms towards heaven and says: "Saint Jude, papa, I am counting on you, my son is in your hands!"

TiJan and Tika decide to stay until Steve is back from the operating room. Paul and Sandra speak with them in the hospital cafeteria.

- *Monchè*, says TiJan pensively, children are extraordinary beings: They make you happy, they make you mad, they make you fear, they drive you crazy. They do a lot of things, even when you don't agree with them, you still love them. You are always on their side, whatever. You can't quit your job as a parent! I would give my life so my son wouldn't have to suffer.

- It's true, Jean, agrees Paul, children are a treasure who cost their parents a lot of emotional sacrifices. It's not a joke I tell you!

-And material sacrifices, interjects Sandra condescendingly, especially when the parents do not have the means. In the financial situation you are in, Steve should never put himself into a position to make you spend money you don't possess. Now, he should give up his plan of going to Harvard!

- What are you talking about? protests Paul. There's nothing that prevents Steve from recovering in two weeks. Oh, where did you get the idea that he had to drop his plans for Harvard? Steve is the first Bonplezi to enter Harvard. And, the way he is heading, he is going to knock them dead at Harvard. He is so very bright. Wait and see.

- For us, declares TiJan, it's a dream that will come true.

Meanwhile, Tika is silent, with her hand on her chin, she sighs, her legs shaking side by side as if the pain is too great for her to stay still. She has a huge load on her mind. It is not Sandra's jealousy that she is worried about...She has not for a minute forgotten about Steve during all of this talking. She is praying. She looks at Paul with tears in her eyes, and says:

- Paul, how long will the operation last? I am afraid of doctors. Sometimes you see them joking in the corridors, acting like teenagers. Some of them who are going to operate rush out to get a hamburger and french fries before they go into the operating room... like school kids... sometimes I wonder if they are really competent...

- They are competent, sister1... They are good. A doctor who works here has to be good. A doctor who operates here has to be good. Believe me. Steve is in excellent hands.

- Well, if you say so, I have no choice but to trust you. You know if they are competent. You also know what is good for your family. But it's hard for me to sit here and imagine that a doctor will be cutting into my boy's flesh. His performance will determine whether my son lives or dies. Oh, Saint Jude!...

- "My boy's flesh!" repeats Sandra, disgusted... You're talking as if Steve as a boy is more important than a girl. Please, Tika! protests Sandra, stop it! You have to realize that it's not the doctor who is going to cut into Steve's flesh, it's Steve who made a mistake and cut his own flesh in this accident. Now the doctor is going to try and fix Steve's mistake. Get that clear in your head, Tika!

- You don't understand, Sandra. I am not comparing him to a girl, I'm just saying he is my darling. I really became a woman when I gave birth to him. Sandra, you have three daughters right? Do you know what a mother's suffering really is? It's like a sensitive cable that connects you to your child. Are you sure you understand when a person tells you she loves her children? It's a feeling that can make you rush into the streets head first like a madwoman or explode with happiness like firecracker.

The surgeon appears. He comes to tell the family the operation is over and was a success. Steve has a broken leg and his neck was sprained badly in the accident but he is going to be all right before the end of the month. They fixed his bone and gave him support for his neck. At least that's what TiJan and Tika were able to understand from the doctor's scientific words...

Let Steve sleep now; don't disturb him until tomorrow morning. That part of the doctor's order is clear to them.

The family is about to leave the hospital when a nurse calls them to come pick up Steve's belongings and blood-drenched clothes. The sight of Steve's clothes with his blood all over really upsets Tika. They return and get to see Steve in his room again. He is sleeping. The nurse encourages them to go home and return the next day, when Steve will be awake. Tika breaks out into tears when she sees Steve lying in a deep sleep that reminds her of death.

- Look at my son! Look at my son, Saint Jude! Look at his blood all over his clothes. My son's blood! My God, look, look, look, look at my son's blood still fresh on his clothes!

- Well, asks Sandra mockingly, where was Saint Jude then?

- Tika *machè*, Paul tells his sister-in-law consolingly, starting today, Steve is somebody who has become even more special than he was, because you have suffered more for him. He is a child who also will bring great joy to his family, you hear. Continue to pray to Saint Jude. In my dream and from what I know, happiness will shine on you and fill your life after this suffering, do you hear, sister!

- Thank you, Paul, responds Tika gratefully, thank you, *frè m cheri*, you give me courage. You are a good old brother.

Tika and TiJan return home to rest. They have to go take care of the two other children at home and reassure them that their older brother is going to be all right. Tika and TiJan get into their car and drive back home. Paul and Sandra get into their own car to go to their home too. On the road, Paul speaks to Sandra firmly. It's time to clarify his position unequivocally.

- Sandra, I find you insensitive towards Tika and that disappoints me.

- How do I lack sensitivity? What am I supposed to say? Her son is wild. He was with that Milton boy. They got into an accident. Everybody knows that white kid is headed for trouble... He is Steve's best friend. So? Tell me who your friends are and I'll tell who you are!

- Steve is not a bad kid, Sandra. He isn't into anything bad. You know this is part of growing up; it's a phase he is going through: He has to make friends and go out with them. He can't seat home all day. Kids want to make decisions. Sometimes, they make mistake. It's when they get burned they realize their parents were right.

- Look at the way you defend him! It sounds as if you want to adopt him!

- I have already adopted him, Sandra. The real adoption is not the one on paper. It's what you feel for the kid. I'm not going to hide it, Steve is a very special nephew to me. I can't do anything about that, I do not want to destroy my feeling for him. And nobody, do you hear me, nobody has a right to meddle in this! Message clear? Stay out!

Paul is really angry. He cannot stand the way Sandra is talking about Steve. He wants her to get a clear and firm message about that.

- Listen, Paul. Don't you raise your voice at me, you hear!. Do you see how that boy is causing problems between us! He is a curse!

- No. He is not. Have you ever asked yourself what do you have against that innocent kid?

- Innocent, innocent! I can't stand him!

Sandra loses control, and shouts very loudly at Paul. She feels terribly jealous of Steve and doesn't even understand why.

Meanwhile, Paul is so angry that he is speeding over the limit. He almost gets into an accident on the highway as the car turns in a curve. Sandra gets frightened and screams at Paul.

- Paul, why are you speeding like that? It seems you want to kill me for that little good for nothing! You don't have to kill me. When I get home, I can pack my bags and return to Haiti with my children. My family will welcome me back with open arms. Besides, they have always told me so...

- Sandra, don't push it further or I'll make you get out of the car!

Can you imagine if Paul made her get out of the car in the middle of Highway I-95 in Miami, with all the cars speeding by...!

# CHAPTER 3

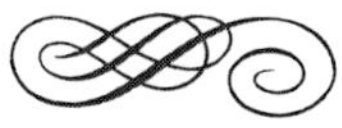

## Tika Today, Sandra Tomorrow

A couple of days after Paul and Sandra had that argument on the highway, they calmed down again. Meanwhile, Steve is recuperating. Tika has been running back and forth to the hospital every day... A lot of relatives have been calling to ask about Steve. Sandra has forgotten about being jealous. She called Tika once to hear how Steve is doing. Tika was very grateful for her call. After all, Sandra is part of the family. Nobody can change that.

One thing that caused Carmen to feel very happy was a call from Solanges, one of TiJan's younger sisters, who lives in Montreal. The telephone keeps ringing in Steve's hospital room. Tika usually picks up the call.

- *Allo*? Carmen, it's Solanges. How is Steve?

- Oh, Solanges, what a surprise, sister. I am so happy to hear from you! *Mezami*, did you hear the trouble we are in?

- I got the news. Paul called me last night and told me about the accident. I am so sorry. I called the hospital immediately but they didn't let me speak with Steve. How are you all? How have you been able to keep up with this situation?

- *Machè,* we are here as you see. Thanks God and in Saint Jude's name, everything is okay. Steve is getting better even though he is still being watched closely. Oh, Solanges, it's so hard to see a child suffer!

- I can imagine how you feel. If, myself, I feel bad although I am so far away. I imagine you feel much worse. You know, Steve is my favorite. I was telling a neighbor of mine what a handsome nephew I have and how incredibly intelligent he is...

- Oh, Solanges, you breathe life into me when you say those beautiful words! For a mother, her son is always handsome but when somebody else sees that, it's a confirmation.

- And how is TiJan?

- Well, he is hanging in there. He is doing better now. To tell you the truth, we almost lost our mind! Thanks God, and with Paul's help, we are strong now. *Machè*, I am always so happy to hear your voice. You're always the same. You keep up your French so well and you haven't lost your Haitian accent either. If I don't practice French with you once in a while, I'm sure I would have forgotten this language completely by now. You know how the children have a tendency to always want to speak English.

- That's the way it is, that's the way it is, Tika. One has to adapt to the reality you're in. As for me, I have a lot of trouble with saying two words in English. So difficult!

- But you are such an intelligent person, and so strong, Solanges. Steve took after you. You both are gifted and you also have common sense... Wait a minute... Steve is now awake and he wants to speak with you. He wants to speak with his godmother. Here you go, son.

- Hi, Aunty Solanges, how are you?

- *Allo*, Steve! How are you? Tell your godmother how do you feel?

- I am well, Aunt Solanges, I want to get well soon so I can concentrate on my college paperwork. You know I have been accepted to Harvard?

- Oh, really! That's no joke, Steve! That's wonderful! Congratulations! My dear godson, how proud I am of you!

- Dad tells me he might let me visit you in Montreal during Summer, before going to college. I can't wait. I'll be able to practice my French too.

- Oh, really? I am looking forward to your visit. That's wonderful news! When you come, we can go on a trip to the Laurentian Mountains. Promise!

Tika gets closer to Steve's bed and stretches over to take the phone from him. She is concerns not to abuse of the pricy long distance call. However, before she let Solanges go, she must ask...

- Let me talk to Solanges, Steve...Hello, Solanges, what's the news with you? Tell me about yourself. I know this is a long distance call. I don't want to keep you on the telephone too long but we have to have a little chat, woman to woman. Tell me, what's new, no prospect yet?

Solanges doesn't say a word. She knows where Tika is heading. She just makes a little sound from her throat to say no. She just listens to Tika, unwilling to engage in the subject but, Tika continues talking. Solanges makes that little sound from her throat again. Tika seems to get it by now.

- Nothing yet! An important lawyer like yourself! All day long you come in contact with big shots, it's impossible that none of them has noticed the great person you are. It could even be a white man after all.

Solanges makes another noise from her throat, she really doesn't want to talk on the subject. She has no boyfriend, she has no boyfriend! Nothing to elaborate about that. However, Tika is too passionate to marry her, she doesn't realize the depth of the discomfort she causes in Solanges. She thinks she is being thoughtful and continues to insist.

- I hear some of those Canadian men make good husbands, sister. Check it out...

-Yes, *machè*.

Solanges is very vague, but Tika wants to see her married so bad that she blindly carries on with the subject. Solanges again makes a sound from her throat. Tika continues. She keeps talking about what's on her mind.

- It's not for lack of my prayers. I pray for you, Solanges, every day. Don't ever be discouraged, you hear. Saint Jude always listens to me. It is going to happen for sure. God is going to do that for us. I tell you, on that day, I will be wearing hat and gloves.

What an innocent pain Tika can be!

Solanges decides to put an end to the conversation. Even though she knows Tika is insisting out of good intentions, she has no patience to pursue the subject now. She interrupts Tika.

- No, Tika, you won't have to dress so elegantly!

- Why, is it out of style? I've been praying for twenty years for that to happen. When it happens, I am going to light a candle to Saint Jude, I'll tell you.

- Good Tika. *Bon*! I am going to hang up now, I am always so happy to talk with you. Don't worry about me, ok, sister. I am fine with my single life. I'll talk to you soon again. Keep up your courage. Say hello to TiJan. *Bisous, bisous.*

- Thanks for the call, Solanges. We'll talk again soon. Remember to pray to Saint Jude. He will take care of you, I am sure. Oh, wait a minute. Jean wants to say a word to you.

Tika hands the phone to TiJan. TiJan is pleased, very pleased that Solanges called and he wants to thank her personally. It's a question of good manners, you know.

- ...Of course, Solanges, we are very touched by your call. We see you don't forget us. You care for us. Thanks for the solidarity, sister. So, everything else is okay?... Steve? Oh, he is doing well now. It's just those cuts on his face that worry me... Okay then, we'll talk again later. *A bientot...*

Meanwhile things are getting worse between Paul and Sandra. They had new arguments again. Paul had gotten very angry. He has decided to have his schedule changed; he has started working at night. He has substituted with a friend. Now, he has created a good reason to never be at home because Sandra upsets him too much. He doesn't come early in the morning after work. He comes at mid-day to change and he returns to work right away. He keeps in touch with his children by telephone and he visit them after school, focus on their homework and, return to work.

Sandra is furious at this new change. At the same time, she's scared. This is the first time Paul does not give in to her whims. She realizes that Paul really loves Steve and he is not going to tolerate that she attempts to mistreat him. But, could it be something else...? In order to find out exactly what is going on, Sandra calls a friend, a nurse who works at the same hospital as Paul. She confides her worries to the nurse who takes her into a wild world of imaginary hypothesis. The conversation has been going on for ten minutes. Let's take a bite.

- You know, dear, what angers me the most is to visualize the person who is the reason for the argument. We are arguing over one nephew good for nothing born in Brooklyn who has no style and no manners. He is now in Little Miami, dreaming of college. If he ever makes it... Hahahhah!.

-You know, Sandra, most men love their family. They have a special bound with their mom and dad as well as with their siblings. It doesn't matter if their relatives wears rags and flip flop. They don't accept that we mistreat them. It is normal, you know, since they are from the same blood.

- Well, if it's that normal for Paul to have a special bond with that nephew, wouldn't it be normal that this nephew be nice to me? Wouldn't it be normal for Paul to kindly explain to me how much these people mean to him even if he is no longer in their social circle? He could have found a way to explain that to me, non? I would have understood. Maybe. I could even have made believe that I love the little monkey. You know, I don't think that what the problem is. Actually, my friend, I am now convinced of something else. The nephew is not the problem. Surely there's a nurse at the hospital, some old white hag trying to make him feel important.

- How come you know so well what's going on?

- What? You mean Paul has a mistress?

The nurse is in shock. What is Sandra saying? She didn't mention the word mistress. In what kind of trouble Sandra wants to get her? Without saying goodbye, the friend hangs up. This topic is too hot and she smells danger. This gossip can cost her her job . She leaves Sandra bathing in rage and stung to the core.

Now, Sandra thinks she understands the reason for Paul's new schedule. A mistress? Oh, no!

So, Paul has an affair at the hospital, she thinks. That's why he doesn't come home even on daytime. That's why he is always so moody. It's not work that is on his mind at night. Aha! Things are worse than she thought.

Wild with anger, she calls immediately her parents in Haiti and tells them with certitude that Paul has a mistress.

Her parents got very upset, especially her mother who has always looked down on the low class family Paul belongs to. Her father tells her to pack her bags and come straight home to Haiti with her children. That the price she is paying for marrying a *Bonplezi.* Where did she meet that low class man with that countryside last name anyway? She should have known, some names, just hearing them, tell where they are from and where they belong! These *Bonplezis*, they are nothing at all!

Did she lose her sense of taste to marry Paul? Why was she so much in a hurry? How could she think that water and oil could blend easily. And the trashing of Paul continues nonstop.

Her mother tells her to tell Paul *exactly* what *Cassagnol had told the ox* in the folktale.

Sandra calls a travel agency to make flight reservations. She has taken the decision to return to Haiti an hour after talking to her friend. Something tells her, however, that she should go to TiJan's house and spill her bitterness. If she doesn't get to see Paul to let him know what she thinks, at least she will pour out her venom on the rest of his family. She wants Tika especially to know all about it! That retarded Saint Jude slave!

She gets into her car and talks to herself, as she is driving.

- Me, Sandra Maneli, caught in a triangle trap! Me, Sandra Maneli! Just imagine that! Good for me! Now the whole *Bonplezi* family must know *he* has another woman in his life. They're laughing at me behind my back and me, the innocent one, I am completely unaware of the situation.

They must be planning all kinds of plots against me. Really? A bunch of people who are not even of my society. Even Paul isn't. Well, he is going to fall down right where he belongs . He's going to miss his children, I guarantee that. I'm going to take all three of them with me back to Haiti.. He will know who Sandra Maneli is... Now, when I arrive at Tika's house, I am going to pour my bile onto whoever talks to me first. That'll teach them!

She arrives at TiJan's home, furious, her heart beating rapidly. She knocks loudly and impatiently.

Knock...knock...knock.

Tika, unsuspecting and pleased at the visit, greets her as she arrives, with her signature innocence.

- Oh look who is here! An unexpected visit. This is really a surprise! What a miracle! Please come in, Sandra. Oh, sister-in-law, what a miracle for you to come unexpected, please come right in. Sit down next to your brother-in-law.

Even before Sandra seats and TiJan greets Sandra, Tika continues.

-We are going to have some eggplant crab stew together, says TiJan, greeting Sandra. Turning to Tika, he adds: "*Cheri*, set a place at the table for Sandra."

-You didn't have to tell me, exclaims Tika, excited. As soon as I saw her, I knew we would be having lunch together.

Tika, unaware of what's coming, changes the subject immediately. At her house, as soon as someone arrives, Steve is the subject of conversation. Tika starts explaining with lot of detail the status of Steve, his medication' schedule, his new sleeping pattern, the interference of one medicine over the other. TiJan follows Tika in the conversation. Steve does this and he does that. Sandra is listening passively. That Steve bla-bla-bla is going into her head and doesn't sit well with her state of mind. If they have paid attention, they would have seen that Sandra is as pale as a cadaver.

- Sandra, asks Tika, you didn't ask us about Steve. He is completely recovered, you know TiJan and I we realize after the accident how many people care about him. Teachers, fellow students and girls too, they all came and visited him. There was one cute blond with long strait hair... She's got Steve on her mind! I know it!

- Anyway, adds TiJan, I see he is very popular and well loved. That makes me happy. He is somebody who gets along with everybody, White, Black, Hispanic, Asian, Jewish, with everybody.

- See how lucky we are, repeats Tika one time too much. Steve is not even going to have a single scar on his body. From what the doctor says, he is going to be exactly as he was before. People can say what they want, I know it's thanks to Saint Jude. I know the novena I conducted and the candles I lit fixed everything. I am sure of that.... Any way... Sandra, come and eat. The stew is going to get cold.

- I never ate anything like that. I don't like to dirty my hands. Eggplant crab is so messy... But...to be king, I'll try a little.

Tika, Jan and Sandra sit at the table. The air is thick as if a time bomb is ticking. Nobody is comfortable. It is not in

Sandra's habits to walk in to their house like that, without calling ahead. If they had arrived at her house unannounced, she would have let them know about it. At the table, she is sitting beside TiJan coldly. Now, they realize something is wrong. They do not know what to say to her. They just notice that Sandra does not seem to be herself. Tika and Jean try to hold a conversation about the weather.

- Sandra, inquires Tika, tell me how your children are doing. They must have grown, now. It's been so long since we saw them.

- They are well. They keep busy.

- Tika, asks TiJan, have the relatives from New York telephoned? Can you imagine, Solanges called us all the way from Montreal but Nicole and Arnold who are in New York, in the same country we're in, have not called yet to inquire about Steve. Some people are really indifferent.

- That's what I have been saying, agrees Tika. Life in the United States is destroying most of our Haitian traditions. Formerly, even neighbors were like family. Nowadays, even your family can become your enemy. I don't know where we're heading. Anyway, TiJan, I will call Nicole and Arnold. I will inform them about Steve. Steve is their nephew, we're all part of the same family, and they have to know what he went through.

- Say hello to them for me, TiJan tells Tika, disappointed by Nicole and Arnold indifference. I don't like to be ignored. I don't like my family to be ignored. I don't want to talk to them today. I've noticed their indifference for a while now. They didn't call on New Year's day. They didn't call for

Easter either. I am disappointed. Since I have to go for an errand, wait until I leave to call them..

Tika glances over towards Sandra and notices that she is distracted.

- You are not eating, Sandra. What's wrong, *machè*? Why are you like that today? You're not yourself. Is something wrong? Would you like to rest on the sofa for a while?

TiJan is debating if he should stay or leave for his errand. He feels that something is going to happen and Tika shouldn't manage it by herself. Sandra is not visiting them for fun. She is cooking something.

They finish eating. Tika gets up and goes to her sewing room. She needs to mend a pair of jeans for Steve. They are Steve's favorite ones, the latest style. She leaves Sandra and TiJan in the living room. Maybe Sandra has confidential information to share with TiJan. The children remove the dirty plates from the table and carry them to the kitchen.

Tika is mumbling a song, From time to time, she looks furtively in Sandra's direction. She was brought up Catholic but, from the time she was a little girl, she always find solace in protestant hymns, especially in moment like now, as she is forecasting a storm exploding under her roof. She starts singing "No, Never Alone."

One more look at Sandra and it is clear there is something amiss. Since Tika sat at her sewing machine, Sandra has not said a word, neither TiJan. They are waiting for Sandra to start talking. She must have something to say. Neither of them wants to be the cause of the storm they feel approaching.

Just as the rain is ready to fall, the storm is growling, TiJan and Tika are ready. Finally, Sandra, who has been sighing again and again, starts by saying that she doesn't sleep well at night. Then she adds that Paul works night shift only and does not come home in the morning. Finally, she said there is a rumor circulating that...Paul is having an affair!

It is as if the storm had exploded...BOOM!

- Oh no, Sandra, says Tika indignantly, that cannot be true! An affair!? Paul having an affair! May God strike me dead; it's not true! No, no and no! There is no such lifestyle in our family.

Tika drops the pant she was sewing and approaches Sandra with mix emotions.

- Well, I'm telling you. I know for a fact! Somebody told me... She's a nurse at the hospital, a white woman... Anyway, I've already made my reservations, I'm taking all my three children back to Haiti with me. I am moving back to Haiti.

- Sandra, what are you saying? Tika protests. You know Paul. You've been married for over ten years now. Your relationship, like in every marriage, has gone through difficult times. Now, someone steps in your life and says something... You have no proof... And you are ready to leave without even having spoken with Paul! Think seriously, *machè*!

-Yes, I am leaving! And, if he doesn't come home tonight, I will leave without saying a word to him. When he comes home, he'll find the house empty. Naked! You hear? I am going to take all the furniture and empty the house in a day. After all, it's the wife who own the house!

Unable to resist, TiJan joins the conversation. He scratches his head first, not sure of what he is going to say. He has always thought that Sandra is not easy to get along with but he cannot believe that Paul be exasperated to the point of having an affair. An affair?

- Sandra, I personally will speak to Paul, man to man. Let me get to the bottom of this for you, ok? This is a serious accusation. Paul has to face this. Calm down, ok Sandra. Stay with us for a little while. Calm down. We're here with you. We're not going to let you face this by yourself.. Now, tell me everything you know about this accusation. What were you told.

- Well, I was talking with a friend...

- Who is that friend?

- I was talking with a friend. You don't know her. She's in my doctors' wives association tennis club. I explained to her that Paul had changed; that, at times, he acts as if he has a double life... that maybe he has someone else in his life. She reacted surprised that I found out.

- Is your friend Haitian?

- No, she isn't. You don't know her.

- But, comments Tika, isn't that strange that you believe in your friend without verifying with your husband. That person didn't say anything concrete for you to be already packing and leaving, Sandra. You haven't talked to Paul yet. You must talk to him before validating this gossip.

- Don't you see that he's found a way to spend his nights away from home. Surely, he is with that woman now. Anyway, it's better for me to go home now, because, knowing me, I can, in my rage, forget who I am and where I come from, and provoke a national scandal!

- Think about it for a second, advises TiJan. What if what your friend said has no truth to it? What if she was joking? And what if you are too blind to realize how much Paul loves you and that you should invest in addressing what keeping you apart now?

- It's true Sandra, seconds Tika. Paul and you are two people who have everything that you need to make you happy. You have knowledge, luxury and three healthy children who have a great future ahead of them. You are both young with stable finances, you love each other and your family loves you. I don't understand why you are saying all these things.

- Tika, what you are saying now means nothing if he is cheating on me. It's the worst affront that can exist when a man ridicules his wife before society. *Machè*, I should better go back to my country and to my parents. My parents are not anybody. In Haiti, when I get back, I'll work in my father's business and I will put the children in the best schools. I'll let my hair down, and, you hear me, I'll not be single for long. I will find the right party to marry. I will find plenty of big shot doctors dreaming to be the lucky one who will have a beautiful mulatto like me in their arms.

What?

Now that Sandra starts spilling her venom, she cannot stop. She continues her bitter monologue, too focused on her imaginary pain to realize that Tika and TiJan are shocked to hear her reasoning. So she continues.

- ...And, that is good for me! A lesson to learn the hard way. My family didn't want me to marry Paul. I was courted by the Brandets and the Madsenis. These guys were crazy about me. They fought over me. My family wanted me to marry into that category of people, especially because my mother and my father are very well known and respected. They knew I would be treated like a princess.. My mother and Pietra were raised together. They were in class together at *Lalue*. My father used to play tennis with Dimitri's father. I should never, but never have married a nobody from Bois Verna. That a tough lesson to learn the hard way!

Well, things seem to be falling apart. Sandra is hurting TiJan and Tika's feelings and this is not seating well with them now.

- Sandra, protests TiJan who is still trying to keep his calm, I hear what you're saying, and, as you speak, you are making me love my wife even more. I would feel very sad if my wife was ready to dump me so easily. I would want to die if my wife says that I am not a good partner choice for her. I would hate myself, if, while I am working hard to care for my family, my wife is trashing me behind my back. I wouldn't be able to live. I wouldn't walk in the streets and feel proud of myself as I feel now, if my wife is thinking nonchalantly of who is going to be my children's future stepfather. Finally, if I know that my wife wanted to marry a Madsenis or one of the Brandets fellows but end up marrying me, her last unwanted choice, I will want her to go back to them. No need to live a mismatch. Each one of us has a shoe that fits.

TiJan is really angry. He is stung by Sandra's impertinence. Her attitude provokes a ferociousness in his voice as he continues to talk.

- Sandra, don't miss the boat of your life, dear. If every day you live side by side with your husband but you're constantly thinking of the other man you should have marry, you're doomed to a life of frustration. Sandra, sincerely, you put Paul down too easily.

TiJan takes a deep breath. He better slow down if he doesn't want his blood pressure to jump. It is evident he has more to say... He hesitates, not wanting to say too much or to hurt himself, but, he can no longer hold back. Thanks God Tika takes over.

Tika?

- Well, Tika adds angrily, if Paul isn't at your level, I guess you have to leave him. There are a lot of good women from good families of *Bois Verna* who would be happy to be loved by Paul. I have to tell you, Sandra, you don't marry a man because of where he comes from, you marry him for who he is, and together, hand in hand, you build a nest. Well, without getting into your private life, since you say Paul is not at your level, tell me what is your level? You. You as an individual. What is it that you bring in a marriage for a man to go crazy for you?

Wow, Tika dares to attack Sandra! Sandra was not prepared for any back punch. Tika and TiJan used to accept anything from her without protesting. What is going on now?

- I am not talking about that, replies Sandra.

TiJan is determined to let Sandra know that this time she has gone too far. He family will no longer tolerate her disrespect.

- No, Sandra, you can't avoid Tika's question. You must answer to her.. You've been aiming a series of insults at this family for a long time and we never said anything out of concern to not hurt Paul's feelings. In regard to the way you treat Paul and his social class I personally never comment because I feel it is Paul who should address this, but, I do have my opinion about it. Today you have cross the line. Right here in this house you came to humiliate our family. Now, that's another thing. That's too much. It is time for you to explain yourself. Now, I am letting you speak. Answer Tika's question.

- There's nothing for me to answer Tika. She isn't even a *Bonplezi*.

Who would have thought Sandra would say something like that? Tika's blood races in her veins and she retaliates immediately! She whips her right hip with her right hand and flips her index finger in the air side to side. With a contortion that could remind you of a snake under attack, she approaches Sandra.

- *Hehey*! Stop right there, Sandra. What did you just say? Did you say I am not a *Bonplezi*? I am a *Bonplezi* with pride and happiness. I am a *Bonplezi*, ever since I left Saint Yves Church, on October 18, 1972. I became a *Bonplezi* for life and eternity. Amen. In the name of Saint Jude.

- Listen to me, interrupts TiJan who is ready to take over again. I am talking to you as a brother. Sandra dear, you have a lot of things going wrong in your head. You don't have self-respect. You don't have respect for the father of your children. You don't have respect for the man who has made you "the wife of a doctor" so you can parade in the exclusive clubs of Miami repeating stupidly how high class you are from head to toe.

You don't have a sincere and honest relationship with nobody, only because you perceive yourself above humanity.

- How can you say I am not honest? I never had an affair! I never cheated on Paul!

- But your mind cheat over and over on him, replies TiJan. When you close your eyes, you are in the arms of the Madsenis and the Brandets!

- And, you should add, TiJan, there is no guarantee that those people really want Sandra, Tika says bitingly.

- Who do you think I am?

-The person you are! Tika and TiJan both answer in unison.

Sandra feels cornered. She has met her match. She came to spit on those people but now they are attacking her. She feels that she is losing ground, slipping in dangerous direction and about to lose the match. She must retract.

- Have you decided to gang up on me for that man? Sandra asks timidly.

- Paul is not "that man," he is your man! replies Tika reproaching. Her tone of voice clearly indicates that she is outraged and she is not going to be intimidated anymore.

- You had plan that attack on me long time ago?

- What do you mean "we have planned that attack?" asks TiJan.

-You have planned to attack us for long time and you have been doing it since you was cursed with that Bonplezi name. You want us to pay for you to have honored us with your noble presence in this humble family. No? What kind of rage is yours, Sandra?

Sandra is angry, bitten, cornered, outraged and scared. She has never been challenged like that in her entire upper class life. She has never been in such a vulnerable situation. Something inside of her wants her to slap these two, but, not only she can't because for the first time, they're showing her their muscle, but also she has no idea what is really going to happen beyond this climax. She has no choice than to play the victim. She feels like crying. She is not used to having people answer her back. She feels she has been caught in a trap and she panics.

- You hate me. You never loved me. She said, as a feline who need to be cuddle.

- We love you, replies Tika in a cold voice, but we no longer want to hear your nonsense! Stop saying that you are superior to us. You're not. Open your eyes. Look at each one of us. We are in America. The country where you get what you invest. And you are investing nothing, dear. Nothing but venom!

- These people have decided to band together to strike me! I have to call for help!

- You can call for help if you feel like it, TiJan says, coldly. But, I warn you, if the neighbors hear you scream and call the police, you are the one who will be arrested. In my house? You come to insult me? You will be arrested! I'm telling you.

Sandra start weeping bitterly. She has lost the battle. She is beside herself.

# CHAPTER 4

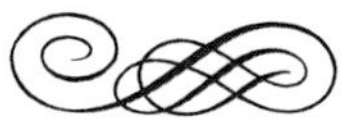

## Love is Priceless

Since Sandra's last scene at Tika's house, life has gone back to normal. TiJan had taken her back home and she didn't resist getting into his bitten *Toyota Corolla*. Since then, nobody has called her to inquire if she went to Haiti or stayed in Miami. TiJan and Tika have no idea if she made up with Paul or not. Every time the phone rings, in the expectation to hear her voice, Tika reacts, saying "Mercy upon us!" as if she is asking Saint Jude for strength and wisdom. But Sandra has not called.

For a few days, Tika has been anxious to talk to Nicole, TiJan's other sister who lives in New York and has not attempted to inquire about Steve wellbeing, although they know he has been in an accident. She has expected that call that never came. So she called herself.

Tika picks up the receiver, dials Nicole's number. The telephone rings for a while.

Ring.....ring......ring.

- It seems they are not home.

And the phone continues to ring. Nobody answers.

Ring ...ring...ring.

-I am going to leave a message, she thought.

Finally, Nicole answers.

- Hello, hello? Oh, Tika, that's you! What's up? Oh, wait a minute, I have another call on the other line.

Tika waits at least five minutes. She waits on and on. Finally, Nicole picks up again.

- Yes, Tika, what's new? What a nice surprise!

- I am ok. What about you? Tell me about yourself? Are you still managing two jobs?

- Yes... Well, you know. I have to... Sometimes, I leave home at three in the morning to start at King's County Hospital for my twelve hour shift. Then, at eight I go to work for that agency until midnight. The time I spend home is barely enough for me to catch my breath. When I am home, I am crushed like an overcooked beans soup.

- Listen to me, *machè*, that's not a life. You're tired, you're asking too much of your body...

- Ah! That's nothing I can't handle. Sometimes I am about to leave work and somebody calls in sick. I have to fill in. What can you do, that's life.

- Then you have no time for your family and for yourself. Is Arnold home?

- Of course not. You know in New York, people need taxis all the time. Arnold doesn't have time to come home. Life in New York is like that. It's like a whirligig that never stops spinning. There are only three types of people who can survive in New York: smart people, ambitious people and crazy people.

- Why do you live like that, Nicole?

- Because life is like that in the United States. Look at Choupette. She is going to be sixteen. I have to buy her a car. She can't go to college in the subway. Children give you satisfaction, you have to give them some too. I don't want white people to think my children are just anybody.

- *Mezanmi*! Anyway, I wish you would take it easy and spend more time with your children. Sometimes children need that more than a car. Kids nowadays are in crisis. They need love!

Nicole does not want to hear Tika's old womanly advice, so she puts an end to the conversation.

- Well, Tika, I am so happy to have talked with you. Everyone is fine, I am sure? Bye...

- Fifi, she said in a loving tone, I called you for a reason. I haven't even told you yet and you are already hanging up. No, everybody is not well. Steve had an accident and I am sure you know that. He is still in the hospital. I almost lost my son, Fifi. If it wasn't for Saint....

Nicole already knows what she is going to say and finishes the sentence for her.

- ...Saint Jude! ... Are you still praying that saint? Anyway, you are lucky Steve is fine.

- Fortunately, he getting better now. He would like to hear your voice, Fifi. He asks about you. He misses you. He can't understand why you haven't called yet.

- You know it's a question of money. I don't make a lot of long distance calls. They are too expensive. That's why I have not called.

- What's the point of you and Arnold working so hard if you can't even afford a five dollar telephone bill?

Tika is disappointed. She realized that Nicole is not interested in her relatives, especially in hearing about Steve. She is wasting her time talking to her. She doesn't even telephone her on holidays. She, as blue collar worker, has to make the call!.

- Well, Tika. I'll leave you now.

- Say hello to Arnold, Fifi. Kiss the children for me. I'll talk to you again. I'll tell Steve you and I spoke. You now, call him collect. Charge your call to my phone number. I'll pay for the call, because, we, the *Bonplezis*, we have to stick together. We didn't come in this country to break apart.

- Okay. I'll call during the week. Bye, bye dear.

- Bye, bye, Nicole.

Tika breathes a long sigh that comes from way down in the pit of her stomach. She is really disappointed at Nicole's lack of empathy.

- Well, if Steve had died, is that the way she would have talked to me? Is that the way Nicole would have cut me off? *Mezami*, that's a disaster. Nicole can't even spend a few dollars to call her nephew... What does Saint Jude say about something like that? I know I am not well educated, but, the way I was brought up and the way I knew the *Bonplezi* family back in Haiti, money has never been the most important thing in our lives.

Tika hadn't quite finished thinking about Nicole when the phone rang. It's Gaston. I don't have to tell you how happy she is. Gaston is calling to inquire about Steve. He calls frequently to support Tika and TiJan.

Ring...ring...ring

- Hello? Sonson! You, brother you never fail to call us. I am so happy to hear you every time. I can't tell you how happy.

- How is everybody? Tell me how Steve is doing.

- Fine. We are hanging in there. When are you coming over?

- Tomorrow, tomorrow. I have a meeting later on today. According to the grapevine, there may be a big decision coming from Washington tomorrow morning and that might a serious impact on Haiti. I can't miss it. You know I have to chase the news.

-*Monchè* Gaston, have you eaten today? You are always attending meetings, always running here and there. You have to eat something that keep you strong. Have you been taking *Hemoglobine Des Chiens*? Have you taught Margaret to mix raw beet, watercress and coconut juice for you? Beets nourishes blood, you know...!

- Yes, Tika, I am eating well. Don't worry. No, I don't take *Hemoglobine Des Chiens*. The name is enough to turn me off! I don't believe in beet juice cocktail. I have to tell you, sister, that beet juice really doesn't enrich blood. Another thing, people shouldn't take medications without a prescription, Tika. Not even vitamins. That's a dangerous habit. I'll have to get you a book about nutrition so you can become acquainted with the natural nutrients in different foods. Some foods can build up your strength too. Remember that, sister.

- Oh, I will enjoy that book. The children are growing, you know. Obviously, I spend a lot on food but I want to stay away from junk food.

- That's good. Okay, Tika. We'll talk about that again another time. Remember to say hello to TiJan for me. I'll stop in to see Steve at the hospital later on today before my meeting. Keep your courage up. We're all in there with you, okay sis?

- Yes. Thank you brother. Thank you. I already feel so much better after your call. You are our main support, Sonson. We used to have a few good long time neighbors. Now, they have moved away. One moved to a place called Tampa, another in Orlando. They call to try to convince us to move up there, but we don't listen to them because we want to be close to you and to Paul. The children wouldn't like that either because they are so used to you both.

- I am very happy that we live in the same town, but Tika, if one day you have to move, you guys have to make the decision that is convenient to you and the kids... the Tampa area is nice... There is a dynamic group of Haitians up there. Orlando too is a good place. From Saint Petersburg to Clearwater, it's quite nice. Haitians do well there... but they are not that many, from what I hear.

- Well, we will visit them but we won't move. We prefer the Miami area. Besides, it's easier for the older folks to travel from Port-au-Prince.. In less than two hours, they land. Your father and mother are getting old; we can't live too far away from them.

- That's true! Okay, Tika, talk to you soon. Say hello to Jean for me.

- Bye, bye brother. Remember, don't stay hungry. If you are ever hungry, come over. We always have something tasty for you.

- Thanks, sis. I won't forget. Good bye, Tika. Thanks again.

Meanwhile, Paul continues to spend his nights at the hospital. There are a lot of patients on his floor and a lot of surgeries to perform. He keeps himself busy. He has been literally living at the hospital and rarely going home. Paul is a very easy going person. He is always happy. Besides the friction with his wife, he calls his children every day at three-thirty. He knows they are home from school and Sandra is not. He has been avoiding talking to her. It seems that Sandra never left nor has she made a scene in front of Paul as she had wanted to.

Things have been going on like that for three weeks. His heart feels so much lighter since he doesn't go home to hear Sandra's nonsense, but he would like to see the children and spend more time with them. Sometimes, the children themselves call him at the hospital. They ask when he is coming to pick them up to go out some place. I must say Paul loves his wife too and he is beginning to think of going back to his regular life with her and the children.

Sometimes Paul seats still, meditating and thinking for long period of time about his life while in the hospital. He daydreams about his family. He thinks about when he was a child in Haiti, how simple life was. He thinks of when he used to spend his vacations in the city of Miragoâne where his parents are from. Oh, that was the good life. He realizes it has been a long time since he has talked to his father, and he hasn't taken time to call to find out how is mother is.

He realizes he doesn't even know how his folks are in this motherland of Haiti. He hasn't spoken with Gérard, his other brother, the teacher who still lives in Haiti. He thinks of all seven of his brothers and sisters and he wonders whether he who has more money and more education is the happiest of them all.

True, all doors are open for him. He goes wherever he wants. He changes cars every year. He has a beautiful wife and three lovely daughters but it seems something is missing. He is bothered by the way Sandra treats him and his family. He wonders whether Sandra really loves him or whether she loves him for his financial situation. He acknowledges that at times, in moment of vulnerability, he had confided to her some of his family's secrets. He had criticized his own family with her, but he never uttered a word of disrespect towards them and never allowed her the right to belittle them. He never said anything to make her believe that he didn't love them.

Besides, there is a secret he never told anyone: He always wanted to have a son. He envies TiJan for Steve. Steve is not any son, he is a loving and intelligent boy with a promising future.

He has come to appreciate TiJan and Carmen even more since he has seen how they have raised their children with good principles, even though TiJan and Carmen are not well off and have no college degrees. Yet, they have a lot of principles. Some of their principles are a little old fashioned but so what! Their children are intelligent; they have dream, they are easy going and not demanding. They are proud to be Haitian. They have a great future ahead and more importantly, a great heart. They are a real blessing. Moreover, TiJan and Tika get along very well, like two peas in a pod. Lot of love and respect.

Paul also remembers how TiJan had worked two jobs when he just moved in the United States. At one of the two places, he worked for six years and never told anybody about it because he was too embarrassed to let people know what kind of job it was about. He was embarrassed because he had finished high school and studied accounting in Haiti, but all that was useless for him in the United States. He was a blue collar who had to find his way in this country. He had to take care of his family. He has to apply for his siblings. He has to send money back home to his aging parents.

Paul remembers how TiJan and Tika had sent for him to the United States and given him every financial support he needed because they wanted him to take the American medical equivalencies examinations, so he could practice medicine here. Thanks to them, he had been able to become a medical doctor in this country.

He was thinking about all these things sitting in his office. As the reminiscence went deeper, the thought of Tika came in his mind. Tika, his sister-in-law, is like a big sister to him. Poor thing, she hadn't gotten a lot out of life, she always work, and work. She works for her family. She helps others too. She probably never received a bouquet of flowers in her life. Where would TiJan get the money for that, even if he wants to treat her?

Paul decides to surprise Tika. He gets the idea to make her happy. First, he calls a florist and orders a big bouquet of flowers for her. As a message, he asks to send the following message in a card clipped to the bouquet: "You are the best big sister in the world."

When Paul supposes that the bouquet has been delivered, he will pay her a visit. He knows Tika will be surprised and happy.

Two hours later, Paul visits them. When he gets there, the bouquet has still not been delivered. Tika and TiJan are sitting in the family room talking. Those two really enjoys each other's company, he thinks. Tika opens the door for him. They both welcome him with open arms as always.

- Paul, what's new? TiJan asks.

- Here I am. How are Steve and the girls?

-They're doing fine, brother. How are you?

- Let me go make you some coffee, says Tika. I bet you didn't get any sleep last night. You work too much, my little brother.

- It's true, sis. I haven't slept. Go ahead and give me some coffee, please. I will savor it with pleasure.

- In the meantime, lie down, Paul. That blue sofa is comfortable. You must be tired. Come and lie down, brother. I'll bring you the coffee along with some grenadine juice.

- Tika, says TiJan, enthusiastically, bring me some grenadine juice too. I'll join Paul.

- How could I forget about you, TiJan! You know I will make you some as well.

- That's what I like about you two, comments Paul. You and Tika are still in love. It doesn't seem like you have been married more than twenty years.

- Yes, agrees Tika, always proud of her marriage, we have been together all that time. It's not every day that things go well but I have a big picture of Saint Jude in my room. When things are not going smooth, I go and speak to him. I always put everything in his hands and that's all.

Paul smiles respectfully and keeps on going.

- Anyway, it's beautiful to see you, sis, Paul tells her.
The doorbell rings. Tika leaves everything and goes to the door. She opens it. Here arrives a man with a big bouquet of flowers in a huge vase to deliver.

- TiJan, Tika calls out puzzled, come here, come quickly. This man is here to deliver that huge bouquet. He may have the wrong address. Do you think it could be for us? It can't be for us!

TiJan gets up and goes to the door to talk to the delivery guy. Paul, still sipping his coffee, is following the scene.

- My word, that's an extravagant bouquet! Where did it come from? It cannot be for us!

By now, Tika has the vase in her hand. The delivery guy is gone.

- The man said is for here, explains Tika. He made me sign a paper. I am going to get my glasses to read what the card says. I don't know where it comes from or who it is for. Paul, can you read it. See what this is. I am lost. I'm not even well dressed in case I have to take it to the next door neighbor if it belongs to her. Paul, you too, help me. See if it's for one of the neighbors. I don't want any trouble with my neighbors, you know.

Tika doesn't understand what's going on at all. She never received flowers before. Nobody ever sent her flowers. There is no reason for anyone to send her flowers. It is a mistake. And yet something in her says, "What if it is for you?" She doesn't know how to react. She sweats. She is thinking that she is not well dressed. Her hair is not combed. She doesn't know what to do. Her emotion overwhelms her.

TiJan reads the card, frown, smiles and steps back.

- Tika, the card indicates your address. It must be for you.

-How can you say it's for me? We both live here, TiJan, come and read the whole thing. You know how I am, when I get emotional, and my heart beats fast. I can't see well, my eyes are full of tears. This would be the first time in my life I would receive flowers. What's the occasion? TiJan, look and see if they are really for us. We don't want to take what is not ours...

TiJan looks at the card again so he can be sure. He is both stunned and amused. He gives it back to Tika. He too is moved by the gesture.

-Well, that's a surprise. Tika, you have to read it yourself. I won't tell you.

Tika, besides herself with emotion, doesn't know what to say, how to behave. It is such a big deal for her, to receive flowers. She finally reads the card. She shakes with emotion. Her eyes fill with tears.

-Oh, TiJan, is it you who sent me this bouquet? Oh, my God! I'm so pleased! Help me, Saint Jude. Help me read the card again. Oh, it's written in Creole. How do Americans know how to write in Creole? Listen, "You are the best big sister in the world." Paul!

Now, Tika is in another world of joy.

- Tika Joseph, exclaims Tika, Tisiyad's daughter, me, poor people from *Derrière Lagon*, in the countryside of *Aux Cayes*, married to TiJan Bonplezi, me, Tika Joseph, Jean's wife, receives flowers today? I got flowers? Flowers? She got flowers! Oh, St Jude! What a day to remember!

She finally understands the flowers are for her.

- No, Paul. Paul, my brother? You sent me flowers? What a beautiful gesture! What a surprise, bro! What a beautiful bouquet! Those are flowers for a president's wife. That isn't any ordinary bouquet. Wow, I am really happy. Paul.  Paul, I have always loved you, Paul. You didn't have to send any bouquet for me to love you. But, this one really makes me feel alive. I am not going to sleep tonight. Or I am going to dream I'm a princess.

- Paul, adds TiJan, we appreciate that gesture a lot, brother. It's a gesture I have never been able to express with my wife, especially raising children with a tight budget, you understand. She knows my whole life is dedicated to her, because she is a good wife and that's what I always dreamt of. A good wife.

- Machè Tika, Paul says to her, I think you are a good person. It's my whole family that salutes you. By marrying you, TiJan made a great choice. TiJan made the best choice!

Tika stands speechless, internalizing Paul's words.  Great choice!  Best choice!

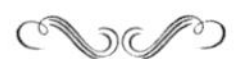

What nobody realized is that the bell had already rung twice. Sandra was driving by Tika's street and saw Paul's car. She parked. She walked in with the intention to overhear what the family was plotting against her. She rang but nobody answered. She walked in and passed the front door. She was heading toward the living room while they were talking. At first, her combative attitude softened when she realized they were not plotting against her. But when she heard Paul say TiJan had made the best choice, her brain wanted to explode. That was too much, so she decided to show herself and surprise the threesome.

- What is all this about, Paul? Who is the best wife?

- Sandra, what are you doing here? Replies Paul, surprised.

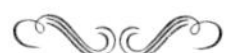

While Sandra and the rest of the family are in Miami and the conversation continues to boil about who is the best wife, other members of the family are treading in the snow of Chicago, of Canada and France. It's not everyone who can enjoy the warmth of Miami during that month. Let's take a trip to Montreal, in Canada, to the home of Solanges Bonplezi. Do you remember Solanges, the lawyer, Steve's godmother?

Today, Solanges is feeling romantic. For you to understand why, you have to be able to imagine life in Canada during winter. Imagine, at the end of October, one day, you wake up and look out the window and everything is covered in white with snow. That's because snow has fallen all night and all day long. A fine frozen powder all over your neighborhood announces that you might hibernate for the next six months or, you might be disconnected from social life until spring, or, maybe, summer. Winter is a challenging season.

In Canada, winter is a beautiful season. The streets, the cars, the houses, everywhere is covered in white. The country becomes a spotless angel, without sin. But that is not all. Go outside and you'll see for yourself. It's the beginning of a cold spell, and a long one too. Winter seats in and it's cold everywhere. Everyone turns the heat on in their house. Everyone has to keep their heart warm too. The cold is ruthless. It goes through your bones. It makes your bones shake as if you were anemic. Canada enters into the tunnel of winter and if you're not a fan of winter sports, you are doomed to survive a semester of loneliness and solitude.

Solanges' home is heated, of course. She lives in a nice condominium in the Outremont area of Montreal. A beautiful neighborhood...

Solanges' home is heated! Yes, *monchè*. And well heated!

It's Solanges' heart that is cold. Her heart has no heat. Her heart is chilly. Her heart is frozen like a piece of ice. Her heart needs love.

Solanges is a romantic. She loves life. She loves music. She loves poetry. She loves love but there is nobody in her life to love.

Solanges is like many educated Haitian women who study for a long time to build a career, secure a future. One day, they look all around and notice they are lacking something. Something essential for happiness that could also soften their hearts.

When Solanges was younger, she was in love and for long time. One day her boyfriend travelled abroad. After six months, she never heard from him again. He met someone else and married her, just like that. Tst...! Forget about that. This has been a pill hard to swallow.

Solanges who is lovesick today is a person who always has made time for others. She is a very well-known lawyer in Montreal. She is also well respected, but, she is in love without anyone to love. Most of the time, life goes on but sometimes, her solitude weighs upon her.

This morning, she is still in bed, the morning program of Radio Canada awakes her. Usually, she enjoys it. No today. She doesn't want to hear the voices of Joel Lebigot or Francine Grimaldi. She has no interest in finding out what is in the news. She would like to listen to music for the heart, something to warm her up.

She puts on her favorite music and gets back under the sheets. Inspired, a poem comes to her imagination:

Life is beautiful, the world is trembling
Love is falling asleep, winter is coming.
Like the flowers and their petals,
The cold is blowing me away. It's winter!

Life is falling asleep, the weather is sighing,
The sky is grey, the world cold.
Outside it is snowing, my heart is freezing,
Despite my struggling, my soul is cold!

I do not know what is happening to me,
This snowy weather softens me.
Silently, it invades my senses,
Lulls me with love and desire.

Oh, how I would like to be in love,
To close my eyes and let my soul

Be overcome with love forever
To savor a taste of the infinite!

Oh, Canada, my beautiful country,
My second land, my second country,
Even though I love you and chose you,
It is Haiti I long for today.
On this snowy white morning,
My heart sighs with nostalgia
It would take a beautiful sunshine
And the warmth of Haiti.

Maybe that is where he lives
The man of my dreams, that handsome black man
Who thinks about me without knowing me,
The one I dream about certain nights.

He would say to me, "Come, darling,
Where were you all this time?
Come to my arms, come closer,
Let me hug you with passion
And never let you go.
Let me make you tremble with love,
The woman I have waited for so long.
Come and let me fill you with chills
And make you cry with love."

I would ask him, "Where have you been?
I have waited so long for you."
He would reply:

"Where were you?
I have looked so long for you?"
(And together we would say):

"From now on, our loving hearts
Will be inflamed with love
At all times, in all seasons
We will conjugate the word love."

Solanges falls asleep again. A tear slides down her cheek to calm her grief. She will be late for work today.

# CHAPTER 5

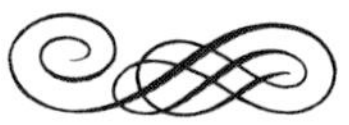

## Everyone has his own grief

While Solanges is falling back to sleep, lovesick and freezing with sadness, here in Miami, you remember, Paul is visiting TiJan and Tika, and *madam* Sandra had just appeared. She had rung the bell but nobody had answered. So she walked into the living room without anybody realizing it. Since everybody was busy admiring the superb bouquet of flowers Paul had ordered to surprise Tika, no one heard when the bell rang, or noticed that she was listening their conversation. She had positioned herself in such a way that she heard what was being said. She always found a way to overhear Paul's conversation.

She is the type of woman who always spies on her husband. It seems as if she is always looking for a reason to argue with him. But this time, the only thing she was able to overhear in the excitement going on in the family room, is the huge compliment Paul addressed to Tika: "TiJan made the best choice." That's what stung Sandra's pride.

She appears angry and interrupts the conversation because she interprets Paul's compliment to Tika as a judgment against her. As if he is saying, that he made a bad choice.

Tst..! There is no comparison. For Paul to think Tika can be a good choice shows that he has no taste at all!

Sandra decides it is time to give them a piece of her mind. Now, we are in the family room with Paul, TiJan and Tika. Let's listen to the confrontation between Sandra and Paul.

- Answer me, Sandra. What are you doing here? said Paul disturbed by this unexpected presence.

- Nothing. What are you doing here? Sandra asks in lieu of an answer.

- I am at my brother and sister's home, that of my nephews and nieces as well. I've come to visit them. Do I have to ask you for permission to visit them?

Sandra is already fuming because Paul's tone of voice is not the one of the conciliatory man she is used to.

- You see, you see what I was telling you, you see the way Paul talks to me, as if he is talking to a maid. You have become fresh, Paul, since you have that mistress. I'm not fooled by you! I know why you are here.

Paul is taken by surprise. He? Mistress? Why he is here? What is he supposed to understand from Sandra's attack? Besides, he really doesn't want to make a scene here at his brother's house where everyone is so loving and caring.

- Tika, TiJan, I'll see you later. I'm gone already. And, Sandra, I don't like those attitudes of yours. Behave yourself, do you hear!

And Paul hits the door as quick as he can, unwilling to carry a conversation with Sandra, conversation that might lead to an embarrassing scandal.

- Paul! You are coming home with me because I have serious business to discuss with you.

- Coming with you? Really? I am going back to the hospital. You better go home. Don't leave the children alone. I don't like that and I don't like your attitude either! Think of what I just said!

- Paul, I don't take orders from you! I tell you I have something to say to you and you tell me you will see me later. You are to take order from me, do you hear? I want to talk to you right away. Come home now, because I am leaving, leaving, I say.

- What are you talking about, Sandra. Leaving for where?

- I am going back to Haiti!

- Back to Haiti? Are you crazy? What's wrong with you?

- I am going back to live with my parents. I am leaving with the children. I am not fooling; do you hear me, Paul? Big trouble, big solution!

Paul is still trying to make sense of the conversation he is having with Sandra. He is half lost, half uncomfortable to handle this nonsense at his brother's house, in the presence of Tika.

- Sandra, calm down. I don't feel like playing. If you have something to tell me, take your time. Calm down. Wait till

I come home. And please, don't come to stir trouble in this house, you hear?

- What trouble am I causing here? This is my house too. TiJan and Tika are my family too. If I have a problem with you, I shall come and tell them about it.

She bursts into tears, sobbing like a little child that has been reprimanded, and continues to talk and sob at the same time. Tika looks at TiJan to get a hint of how to handle the situation but TiJan is looking at Paul in a way that question this type of relationship that he is not used to.

- It hurts me that you are causing me so much grief. I never had any and I don't want to have any. My family doesn't want me to have any. I have never been in a situation like that, Sandra says, between sobs.

- Sandra, what grief are you talking about? Get it out or stop talking that way. What is the grief? Are you sick? Do you have a fever?

- What is my grief? What is my grief, you're asking? Aren't you ashamed to ask me what my problem is? You are my problem. You are causing my grief. You have a mistress at the hospital!

- What mistress are you talking about? TiJan? Tika? What is she talking about?

- Yes indeed, you are seeing another woman and that's why you're moody like that with me.

- What is she talking about? You know, I don't understand anything about what she is saying! Are you dreaming, Sandra? Are you sick? Do you have a fever? Tell me what's wrong with you!

- You are not taking me seriously, Paul. You have a mistress at the hospital, everybody there knows about it and they're all making fun of me. Somebody asked me how I found out…

Paul loses his temper because he has no idea what Sandra is talking about.

- TiJan, Tika, I have no idea what Sandra is talking about. This is absolutely false. This is not true. I don't know what Sandra is talking about. I think she is just looking for something to argue about. I can't take it and I don't want to be part of it. Well, I'm leaving. I am going back to the hospital. Anyway, I'm on call, I can't stay longer. Sandra, I am not going to pay attention to you and your foolishness.

- Paul, Tika objects, you shouldn't leave now. Don't go yet to the hospital. You should call in sick and take time with Sandra to get to the bottom of what she is saying. I can't think of anyone in our family facing such situation. I can't think anyone of us being in this situation. Paul, you know there are diseases you can catch with other women... I wouldn't want to see you hurt, on St Jude's name….

Paul is furious. He feels that TiJan and Tika suspect Sandra is revealing a big secret. He doesn't hope they believe her. That bothers him that Tika could have a bad impression of him and that is the main reason he loses his temper.

- What could happen to me, Tika? I just told you it's not true. I'm through talking. I'm leaving, do you hear!

- See you, brother, TiJan says to him. Take care. Please take care.

Paul leaves. He seems neither angry, nor pleased. He leaves Sandra behind with her imaginary mistress. TiJan, unwilling to take position, wonders what the truth is: Paul does not seem to be the type of man who would have a mistress but you never know. Tika does not know what to believe. She leaves Sandra and TiJan in the living room, goes into her room to talk to Saint Jude. Let us listen to her prayer.

- Saint Jude, papa, you are my patron saint, listen well to me. This can't happen. That woman is crazy, I know, but we can't let Paul do something like that, right before our eyes. Saint Jude, papa, I am asking you to speak to me. If it's not true, bring peace back to the family. If it is true, show your anger so Paul will know, at this time that HIV and AIDS are rampant, it isn't an appropriate behavior for a family man. Listen, Saint Jude, papa. I am asking you this. Manifest yourself in the name of the God in heaven. Destroy every sin among us, in the name of the Lord. Make the earth tremble…

A loud noise is heard, interrupting Tika's prayer abruptly and breaking her heart. Tika thinks the noise she hears is the manifestation she was just asking for in her prayer, and in a panic attack, she loses her mind completely.

- Help! Help! Saint Jude, what answer have you given me?

TiJan runs into the room behind Tika, in response to her emergency call for help, thinking something wrong happens to her.

-What's wrong, Tika?

- *Woy! Anmwe!* Saint Jude has just manifested himself before me. It must be true about Paul.

- Why are you saying that?

- I just finished praying. I asked Saint Jude to manifest himself, to crush the sin if Paul is having an affair and I heard this awful noise as if Saint Jude was very angry.

- Tika! Tika, machè! Of course not! This is not an answer to your prayer. I just dropped a gallon of water on the floor. Sandra had asked me for a glass of water and I drop the gallon inadvertently. Tika, put your head in place. I don't even know if Saint Jude understands Creole, for him to be able to answer you so fast! He has to have an interpreter. Why don't you go and speak to Sandra instead. She is still here. She is crying in the living room. Leave Saint Jude alone... I, myself, I have no idea how to handle this. It seems maybe Sonson is the only one who can talk to Paul... Gaston is better at this…

Tika and TiJan return to the family room to talk with Sandra who is still sobbing like a little girl who has lost her doll. TiJan tells her he doesn't like to see her cry like that. He is trying as he can to help her.

- What can we do for you, Sandra?

- What can you do? What can I do! My family already told me I could return, I am going to take an airplane and go back home. There is nothing you can do for me!

- Sandra, I believe Paul. He says it's not true, assures TiJan.

- He says that, but you see, he wants to stay in the hospital.

- Sandra, *machè*, counsels Tika, listen well to what I am going to say: Don't go anywhere. Stay here with your children. Stay at your home with your children. Take your time. Take a deep breath. Pray. Talk to Paul, but speak with him tenderly, and you will see, everything will return to normal. In our family, nobody separates. Nobody hurts anybody. We are one united and supportive family. We will not allow you to break up your family, ok? I am going to pray for you, do you hear?

In the meanwhile, Gaston just left a meeting. He had to find out what effect the embargo is having on the life of Haitians in the motherland. He had to know if it was going to be intensified or lifted. He must know what turn of events were to be expected in Haiti in the coming days. He knew that everything was contingent on the results of the elections in the United States. Now the elections are over; there's nothing going on.

He is bored. He could go to TiJan's house but he doesn't feel like hearing Tika keep talking to him about marriage or about St Jude. He doesn't feel like going to Paul's either.

He has learned from Tika that the couple is having marital problems and that is not something he cares to mingle with. He decides to telephone the family in Haiti.

Gaston picks up the phone and dials his parents' number. He is always very happy to call Haiti. Whenever he calls, he feels transported in spirit to the *Maïs Gâté Airport.* He almost feels that puff of heat you get as you get off the air conditioned plane at the airplane door. It's the same heat he feels in ManPlezi's arms when she embraces him, when she kisses him twice, three times, ten times, because she is so happy to see him when he travels to Port-au-Prince. Oh, she is a lady, this Marilisi Bonplezi.

As he thinks of her, the phone rings in *Bois Verna*, Port-au-Prince, at the family home. ManPlezi answers.

- Hello! Hello, Mom, it's Gaston, what's new?

- Gaston! My dear son! If you're calling, that means you've some news.

- What news?

- What do you mean what news? You don't know? Well, in this case, let me have you talk to your father.

- Hello, Gaston? Have you heard from Gérard?

- What is going on with Gérard?

- Oo! That's worrisome...! You didn't get any news from Gérard?

-Papa, that's what I just said. I don't have any news from Gérard. What's going on? What's wrong?

- Well, *monchè*, it's funny, I must say. It's funny, because… Well, you know there are moments in life...

Gaston is impatient, he feels something serious is happening or has happened to Gérard but his father is crafting an endless introduction. He cuts him off quickly because he needs to know what the matter is.

- Papa, can you tell me exactly, as clearly and concisely as possible what is going on with Gérard?

-*Monchè*, you are too much in a hurry. As for me, I am really under an emotional shock, because I thought you were calling to give us news of Gérard.

- Papa, what are you saying? Gérard is with you in Haiti!

Big Sonson finally realizes that Gaston has no news of Gérard, he feels his heart in his throat, his big intestines eating up his small ones, and maybe even his blood sugar level rising. He feels his body getting as cold as a block of ice. He senses problems. He imagines Gérard lost. He turns around to speak to his wife, even though he is on a long distance call.

- Marilisi, Marilisi please, give me a grain of salt. I am under shock. It's true, Gaston has no news of Gérard.

- Papa, I'm talking with you, and you are speaking to Mom. You know this is a long distance call. Can you please tell me, I am asking you for the second time, what has happened to

Gérard? Is he sick? Remember, this is a long distance call. This call is costing me a lot. Is Gérard sick?

- No, he isn't sick. He has broken the cord...Oh. my God, this looks bad! And Gwo Sonson's voice melts down in a deep pain.

- He broke the cord? What does that supposed to mean?

- Sonson, what's wrong with you? Don't you understand? He is gone! That's what I am trying to tell you in a coded language.

- What? Is he gone where?

-O, son! What is so complicated for you to get. *Laba, monchè!*

Gwo Sonson is relieved that Gaston finally understands – He is so slow to get it! he thinks. However, Gaston has not fully grasped the message clearly so he makes an attempt to get more precise information.

- Where did he go?

- I don't know, son, he left. He left with Edith and the six children. He left Port-au-Prince to *La Tortue* or somewhere like that. From there, he was supposed to take a boat and join you...

*What?*

The news is too much for Gaston. As he listens, his heart starts pounding loudly. He begins to perspire with fear but he continues asking questions.

- Papa, what are you saying? You are killing me, papa! Are you telling me Gaston is coming to the United States illegally?

- Don't talk that loud, son! You don't have to say everything on the phone. You should not even mention his name. What's important now is finding out if he has arrived.

- Arrived where?

His father is impatient that Gaston still doesn't understand and keeps asking where.

- Where you ask, Gaston? Gérard left. He went over there. You know where. I know when he gets there he will call you. The problem is, I don't understand why he hasn't called yet.

- What day did he leave?

- I don't remember. First, he sold all his things. You know he had lost his job. He came to visit us and started talking about all his griefs and regrets. I tried everything to make him stay. I told him I'd try to get him a job in Biron's office. He refused. He said he was going to try out his luck. He said he couldn't play around with the kids' future anymore.

- Where are the children now?

- I think he said he was leaving with them.

- What! With all six children?

- Even with the baby! He didn't want to leave any of them behind. I don't understand what happen to him but he was stubborn. He didn't want to listen to anything I told him. The timc had come for him to go. Here, let me have you talk to your mother, she wants to talk with you again.

- Gaston, So you have no news of Gérard? How is that possible, son? I was convinced he had arrived and was with you...

- *Mom*, if what Papa told me about Gérard is true, he is in problems, big problems. When people come into the United States illegally, it's like going through the head of a needle, before you are able to get in. I don't know what I can do. Anyway, lct me hang up. I'm going to make a few calls, to try and find out what is happening. I'll call back as soon as I have any news.

- Call us later and let us know what you find out, his mother pleads with him.

- *Mom*, it may take days, weeks or even months before we know where Gérard is.

- What are you saying? If I don't get news of Gérard, I will die!

Gaston hangs up. He feels the blood in his body turning into cold water. It is only after he hangs up that he realizes the situation he is in: his brother, Gérard Bonplezi, is entering the United States illegally. He has always heard about people in that situation and had always wanted in some way to help them. He knows the nightmare people with illegal status go through. He never thought one of his brothers could be in that situation. Gérard Bonplezi, yes! Gérard Bonplezi! This can't be true!

He remembers what he has seen when he visited Krome and the Dominican Republic. Long line of powerless Haitians stripped of their humanity, trapped in a soulless system, treated as pestilential animals, begging for a sip of water and waiting for an unconcerned agent to inform them for how long they will be jailed for the crime of desiring a better life. Gaston felt his blood quiver goose pimples invaded all over his back. A chill went through his body from the bottom of his toes all the way up to the tip of his hair. He felt it passing through his stomach as it went up. He had to run to the bathroom. His stomach has always been his most fragile organ. He ran lose without control. All of a sudden a taste of bile came rushing out of his mouth. That's the echo of his brother's trouble resonating in him.

He tried sitting, standing, walking all over the apartment. He couldn't wake up from the nightmare of that phone call. He keeps hearing his mother's voice asking him to call back later to let her know. But what news can he give her! Where will the news come from?

It takes him a few minutes to rationalize that there could be good news just as well as there could be bad news. Good news maybe if Gaston arrives and is set free by the immigration system. Bad news could be drowning at sea in the middle of the cruel ocean. He cannot stand the thought of this anymore.

Because of the seriousness of the situation, Gaston decides to call Paul first. He dials the number but there is no one home. He calls TiJan and Tika's home. Tika answers and asks him if he has eaten already, why not come over for coffee. He feels there is no point in going to talk to Tika because she can't do anything to help, nor can her Saint Jude.

As he thinks, he remembers Solanges, the sister in Canada who is so far away. He also thinks of Nicole, who is too busy making money and who is not much interested in what's happening in the family. He thinks of calling Antoinette, his younger sister, the actress, who lives in Chicago. She is another one not too easy to deal with...

He decides to call Antoinette, He's got to do it!

He picks up the phone like a man who is holding on to an electric pole during a cyclone when the wind is blowing so hard that metal roofs can fly away, rip you off or cut your off neck. He is like a man in the middle of the ocean in a storm, the water spinning wildly and trying to suck him under while he tries to grab onto a rubber tube. You know it's a hopeless situation. You know it's hopeless but you hang on, hoping for a miracle. You talk to anyone. Anyone who has a soul.

Ring.........ring........ring

- Hello? Antoinette? It's Gaston.

- Hi, darrling, how arre you?

- I'm here trying to survive. I called to tell you know Gérard has left Haiti!

- Good for him. It was time, wasn't it? I couldn't underrrstand why he stayed behind for so long.

- Listen to me well. He is coming illegally.

- What did I hearrr? You don't have to say any more, Gaston. I don't want to hearr another worrd! I don't want anybody arrround here to find out that I have a rrelative who is an illegal alien. I'm glad you called while Henri Claude is out. He doesn't even have to know.

- *Cocotte*, what is getting into your head? I call to tell you that our brother has risked his life and the life of his family to come illegally in this country. I call to share with you that his life may be in danger and you are telling me you don't want anybody to know?

- Ouch, wait a minute darrling. The phone is ruining my earring. Wait till I take it off... Now, listen, this converrsation doesn't interrest me at all. Gaston, I have to go now, do you hearr. I have a parrty to go to tonight and I haven't even starrted getting rready for it. My nails are not done yet, I haven't yet decided what I am going to wearr. Instead of talking with you, I should be at the spa. I rreally have to go now. You are upsetting me.

- *Cocotte*, what if I had called to tell you Gérard is dead?

- Listen, Gaston, don't play with my feelings that way. Gérrard is not dead. Gérrard is coming by boat, just as I took a plane one day. He isn't a child. If he came by boat, he knows what he's doing. Gérrard is not so poor. Surrely, he is coming on a crruise, you must have misunderrstood.

Disappointed and besides himself, Gaston tries to control his temper and tries again.

- *Cocotte*, how can you say that? When was the last time you spoke to Gérard?

- Listen, darrling, I rreally have to go. If the family wants to collect money for him, let me know. I have my life to live. I can't take other people's prrroblems upon me. When you're an arrtist and a model, you have your hands full!

- *Cocotte*, are you or aren't you interested in Gérard?

- Yes, I am interrrested in Gérrard, but I'm not interrrested in what Gérrard is doing now. That has nothing to do with me. I am a perrson who wakes up earrly in the morning for a yoga session. Afterr that, I take a walk. Then, I come home and wait for the masseurr to give me a massage. By then, it's almost time for lunch. Then, I starrt receiving a lot of calls...

She stops to clear her voice and drink something before continuing.

- ... This week forr example, I have an interview for a movie that is being filmed in West Palm Beach. You see, I need peace of mind to be able to concentrrate on those things. I can't imagine the situation of somebody who is coming here like boat people. Think of it, *mon cherr*, just think of it!

No, Antoinette tries too hard to ignore those people in her life. How could she understand their problems! She has made it. She cannot hear the voice of thousands of Haitians dying, suffering, just because they are attempting to enter the United States. It is not her problem. She cannot imagine people with problems. People without an entry visa. People who are not qualified to enter the country. People who are detained upon arrival. People who risk their lives to come in, taking flimsy boats, risking their lives. People who never made it on shore and vanish at sea, becoming a feast to hungry sharks. Even if it is her brother! Sincerely, this is not comprehensible! What kind of people do that?

Gaston cannot understand Antoinette's attitude nor her reasoning while he, every day, he feels the heartbeat of his people, he has his eyes wide open on his people's suffering. His soul is right there, in Haiti or wherever they are beating up his brothers, be it in Krome, the Dominican Republic, the Bahamas, or elsewhere. How can one of his sisters think and feel like that? Gaston who search to understand the pain, the misery and the tribulations of his people cannot understand the cold blooded indifference of Antoinette.

Family is a mystery, Gaston thinks. Brothers and sisters, father, mother, aunts, friends, can think and feel differently from you as if you're not related. As if you have not gone through similar experiences. But *Cocotte* makes him angry; he might as well hang up.

- Bye, darrling. Say hello to Marrgaret.

Tst...! Gaston hangs up without a word.

Gaston puts the phone down and shuts his eyes. He does not know how to start looking for Gérard and where. And yet he has helped people in different type of difficulties before. He has helped people fill out Immigration applications. He has guided people with temporary visa to file for permanent status. But when it's your brother! Besides, he doesn't even know where he is, where to find him, whether he is alive or dead. It is not the same at all. He shuts his eyes and tears run down his cheeks. He thought he would never cry!

He falls asleep. He sleeps in fear and hopelessness. In his sleep, he dreams of Anit, Gérard's eldest. He sees them in the boat. Anit, who must be just thirteen, talk to him in his sleep and says:

-Uncle Gaston, this is what happened:
Father gathered us all
And said we were leaving
We are all leaving, he said
We are taking the road to glory.
Let's go, you the Bonplezi,
We are going to seek for a better future
In the land beyond the water,
We will join the other family members.

When day comes, mother packs all our bags
We leave Port-au-Prince, we go to the province.
We leave the dirt roads and take the corridors
Until we arrive to the Northwest, near *La Tortue*.

We met people on the way, young and old
All are happy, tomorrow we are leaving.
It's like the Carnival, it's like a wedding,
Tomorrow before dawn, we leave Haiti.

We get up real early, at three in the morning,
We did not even get to sleep, we are so anxious
For that time has come.
Papa said to us: Come on, children,
Today is joy day. Today we are leaving.

Mother is silent, with Junior in her arms
Tififi and Patrick holding on to her skirt.

Charline and I are each carrying a suitcase
While Fanfan carries the bag of foods.

The boat leaves at four o'clock in the morning.
The church bell is sounding strangely.
I shiver.
It is as if God is seeing us take off with sadness.

But papa is brave, he feels we are sad
And says, children, come on, come on.

We have no belongings, not even a doll.
Everything is staying behind, at Junior's godmother's.
We take nothing because father says:
We are going, we are leaving, we need nothing.

When the boat sets sail, there are almost a hundred of us
Aboard, like at the Carnival.
Everyone sings: Hosanna, Hosanna!
We don't know the song but it sounds
Sweet to our ears.

When mother sees the boat leaving
She starts singing too, her voice trembling,
As if she is going to cry, but doesn't.
As if she is going to scream, but doesn't.
She shuts her eyes.

Mother says not a word,
She does not even look at us
Like a zombie next to us,
As if she is leaving her good angel back in Haiti.
As if only a piece of her is following her husband.

She is carrying Junior in her arms; he is asleep.
My little sister is leaning against my leg.
The boat starts to rock, rocking back and forth.
Papa looks into the distance, as if blinking to see,
As if he knows where he is taking us
As if he has seen the Promised Land.

The boat is loaded with people,
No room to stretch my legs.

At six o'clock, we are in the middle of the ocean.
When I look in front and when I look behind,
There is no land in sight.
The land has disappeared,
There is only water all around,
In front of me, behind, on the sides, everywhere,
I see only water.
There is no more land.
The land of Haiti said goodbye to us.

I never could have imagined so much water.
I could not have imagined such depth of water.
I never thought the trip could be so long.
This voyage is too long!
When will we arrive?

Suddenly the water gets angry
The Carnival is over, everyone starts to shout.
The boat is sinking! Sinking! Sinking!
I never thought the Carnival would break up this way,
Ending the fun and leaving us capsized at sea,
In the middle of the angry ocean.
I do not even know how to swim, uncle.

I could never have imagined our journey would end here,
In the middle of the angry ocean.
Have we already reached our destination?

Everyone is shouting, the boat is sinking.
People are screaming desperate sounds,
Their eyes out of their orbits.
Death is coming to take us, children and adults.
Hungry sharks are welcoming us.

*Uncle Gas*, we are on our way,
We are coming to see you.
But we will not get there,
The sea is blocking the road.
Destiny has decided, this is where the trip ends.
Our eyes will not cross,
We will not see each other again.

The last time I saw Mama and Papa,
Their arms outstretched to catch me out of the water.
Mama could not tell who out of the six of us
Was drowning and who was floating.

Before closing my eyes to go to where God is,
I think of you *Uncle Gas*, you are a good uncle
I will miss you; I will miss the toys you sent me.

I will miss Haiti,
I will miss the land across the waters
Like in those beautiful pictures,
Oh, what a beautiful place!
I wished I had a chance to walk in its streets.

But the water is mightier...

# CHAPTER 6

## Father and Son

From what we have learned last time, Gérard, Edith and the children are on their way to the United States via a boat. It seems most likely that they are coming to the country illegally. They are coming as boat people. ManPlezi and Big Sonson told that to Gaston the last time he call them. Then later that night, Gaston had a dream, a real nightmare. In his sleep, Anit, Gérard's first born, tells him the boat had sunk. Since then, the family has been waiting for more news. So far, nobody in the family has heard from Gérard.

Steve has left the hospital. He has been home for a week. He is fully recovered. He doesn't even have one trace of a cut on his face. He has just eaten and is ready to go out with a friend. TiJan and Tika have been waiting for this moment to be heard.

- Son, how are you doing? His father asks, to engage in a conversation.

- Better, dad, much better. I feel great. Actually, I am ready to go visit my…

TiJan scratches his head, as if that gesture will give him the courage to lecture his son.

- Well, before you take off, let's talk... I have a few words…

- Oo! Am I in trouble? Should I be ready for a lecture?

- Why not? Steve, if I want, I will lecture you. However, that's not my intention. Listen: first, I have to praise you for being so courageous. You went through a lot, you suffered stoically and recovered so fast! I am proud of you, son. However, I am still in shock. God! You came out of this accident very fast but I am still trying to recover from the fear and the panic I endured to see you in that situation. This accident was no joke, you hear?

Tika joins them in the conversation. She too has a lot to say.

- Steve, my son, you must understand your mother. Whenever your child is in danger, you have the feeling of being in the delivery room again. This accident was no joke, Steve...

Seated next to his mother and facing his dad, Steve realizes how traumatized his parents were from his accident. The tone of his father's voice and his careful choice of wording are unequivocal indicators of fear and sadness. His mother's expressing that her pain was comparable to being in the delivering room again gives him a sense of the pain and the turbulence his accident caused.

He decides to listen obediently to them without uttering a word since it matters a lot to him that he regains their trust. Steve is the type of young man who is proud of his judgment and cares to restore his parent's confidence in him. At the same time, as a young man, he is looking forward to normalcy and can't wait to be with his friends and enjoy his last summer before heading to college. In a softly voice, he addresses their concerns.

- Well, Dad, it's over now, no?

- Not for me, protests Tika. I still feel my insides boiling. Do you think I can ever forget what happened?

- No, it's not over, son, the father agrees. Your mother and I have seen your blood all over you. You were bleeding, my son. It's no joke. We went through the nightmare of seeing you at death's door. Can you picture us at Jackson Memorial Hospital waiting for a doctor to tell us about your fate, you Steve, our beloved son? What if the doctor had informed us you would be paralyzed for life? Do you understand? Do you understand, Steve?

- I understand, Dad. Believe me. I understand and I promise that I will be very careful for the rest of my life. But Dad, can you make it short? I can't take more of this, now. If you want to continue with this conversation, can we talk some other day? Please.

- No, Steve, insists his mother. This can't wait for another day. We have to talk to you now because we don't want this to ever happen again.

- Dad, Mom, can we just forget about this? It was an accident. I promise to be careful, as I said, for the rest of my life. Can't you forgive?

- Forgive, yes, forget, no! The father exclaims. Imagine. You are ready to take off to visit your friends. You are on your way back to the streets. Soon you will be out all day.

I have to talk to you now. Son, there is no escape; you have to listen to us. Car accidents are the leading cause of death among young men in the United States. You were about to become a statistic. You could have died. And your bone, by now, would have been rotting away six feet under. Do you understand?

TiJan raises his voice at the thought of such fatality.

- Dad, please, I am here, alive. Let's don't go that far. I am not dead!

- But you could have been. Your mother and I would have been heartbroken, losing you forever, watching the dream of you going to Harvard fallen apart. Can you understand how precious your life is? Do you realize you are not just another child? You are Steve Bonplezi. Our only son!

- Dad, I promise, I will be more cautious. I will not make you go through that pain any more. Never. Never. Promised!

- You better don't, insists his mother, because I can't be taking advantage of Saint Jude like that. It's not every day answer your prayers. What would have happened if, when I prayed to him, he didn't pay me any more attention? What if Saint Jude had given me no more attention he would have given to a dog? I have no clue what would have happened to my soul.

- Do you understand, pleads Steve, this will not happen again. It was an accident. Is not that I wanted attention and my friend and I decided to be involved in an accident. I know, Mom. I understand, Dad. Now, I know better. I am not a child anymore.

- What I do know is that I want you to be responsible and very careful with the type of friends you are mingling with, his father replies.

- I will be, Dad. You can count on me.

- You will, my son, you will, TiJan assures him. You are born to be a success. I want you to complete college and succeed in life. Your mother and I dream every day about that. I am counting on you. So is your mother. You are too worthy, you are too important to us, you mean too much to us for your life to be put at risk. Don't never let that happen again.

- Gosh! Dad, you make me feel so important. Thank you. This touches my heart. I am really sorry I cause you so much pain. Thank you for talking with me like that. Tell me, Dad, do other parents talk to their children like that?

- I don't know what other parents tell their children, the father replies, and I don't care how they communicate with them, but, it is more likely that all parents love their children, almost always more than they love themselves.

The telephone rings, interrupting the conversation, fortunately for Steve. He couldn't wait for this to end! Although he understands his parents point of view, he felt that they were pounding at him and he was hoping and praying to go take some fresh air out.

Ring............ring...........ring

When the phone rang, Tika left Steve and TiJan and ran to picked up. It was Antoinette, TiJan's younger sister, the one who lives in Chicago. The model who is also an artist. *Cocotte*, is her nickname, you remember. She was the one who carried that awkward conversation with Gaston the other day.

- Well, Tika, what's new?

- What a miracle to hear from you! Where are you calling from, Antoinette?

- I'm in Chicago, darrling, I'm at the studio. I have just signed a contrract with a company in West Palm Beach. I will be down therre soon for a filming.

- Will we see you? West Palm Beach is close to Miami. You can get here in no time.

- That depends. I will be on a verry tight schedule, between filming and dinners. And, I want to see Palm Beach Island too, just acrross from wherre I will be staying. I've been told that it's a gorgeous place. Henry Claude drreams of buying a villa in that arrea.

- Oh, that's good. Things must be going well for you. From what I hear, only big shots live on that island.

- God! (Making a movement) I just brroke the nail of the little finger of my left hand. Oh, my God, how terrrible! That's a prroblem! I am so upset! How will I be able to go to the party tonight with this brroken nail? It's unthinkable!

Tika loses her patience over this story about the broken nail, which she doesn't understand at all.

- Well, *Cocotte*, you break a nail, well, so what! What's a nail?

- Tika, darrling, you don't underrstand. A woman's hand is her passporrt. When the prroducer kisses my hand, he should see and feel that my hand is soft and prretty like velvet. A woman like me cannot walks arround a brroken nail! It is inconceivable, darrling!

Tika loves Antoinette very much, but she always wonders what is the intention of that woman who grows her nails so long, just for attention. There is no way she could even think of such foolishness. Aren't our fingers tools to be used for daily living? Fingers are attached to our hands to clean up house, wash the dishes, prepare food, bathe and eat. What are Antoinette's fingers for?

- Well, *Cocotte*, do you cook? Do you wash dishes? Did you even ever change Hakim's diapers?

- Tika! Oh no! I do not cook. What an idea, dear. Me, put my hands in spices! You arre crrazy, darrling! We have a Frrench lady who cooks for us at home. Hakim's diaperrs have always been the nanny's job. You know, our maids rrun the house. As you alrready know, I am a Frrench doll who is borrn to be spoiled rrotten!

- In other words, you don't know what it is to cook a good dish of sorghum with Congo beans for Henry Claude?

- How does that taste! Sorrghum! Out of question! What would I do if that type of food upsets my stomach?

Rremember I am an arrtist and a model, Tika. You can't forget that. No! Oh no, I would neverr eat something like that. You see, I am in a special diet. Anyway, you won't understand, dear. I have to leave you. I'll call again after the filming, ok? I'll speak with you from West Palm Beach and tell you all about the high society there....

- That will be nice, Cocotte. I have been told there are a lot of Haitians there too. Who knows, you might meet someone you know there.

- I don't think so. We'rre not talking about the same place at all, Tika. I'm talking about the place wherre the Kennedys have theirr mansion, just acrross. I don't think therre are Haitians living therre, for yourr information.

- Excuse me. You know more than I do. Take pictures so I can see.

- I'll ask someone frrom my rretinue to take some picturres. You see, darrling, my schedule is very tight. Anyway, say hello to TiJan and kiss the childrren forr me.

- Ok, Cocotte. Say hello to Henry Claude and Hakim. Bye.

Tika hangs up. She doesn't understand why Antoinette even called. Maybe she called because she was happy to have signed that contract. She seems to care for the family but we are not rich and sophisticated enough for her. Sometimes she tries to approach us, she calls, but, nothing she says makes sense. She is living in another world, with all kinds of big shots and high class people. It seems, even if she had stayed in Haiti, she would have that superior air. What is she going to do over there where the Kennedys live? Why is she going there? Wait and see. She will call us again, just to remind us that we cannot visit her in her Eiffel Tower place.

When Tika returns to TiJan and Steve after Antoinette's call, she sees the two of them talking intimately. She decides not to interrupt. It looks to nice when father and son are entertaining a private conversation, man to man.

You know, you and I have to hear part of it!

- Dad, you know, I am already picturing myself becoming a successful man... I have to make it happen...

-It's good to hear it from you, son.

-Dad, why is it that Uncle Paul doesn't look that successful? He is rich and married, but, he doesn't look happy!

- Well, he has accomplished a lot. Maybe, he needs more support from his wife. Married life seems to be easy but it isn't. The choice of a wife has to be based on deep values and true love. Maybe that is the problem in his case. To love and to marry are two separate things. That is the reason you should insure to give your heart to someone who really deserves it!

- Thank God, I am not ready for that, Dad!

- Anyway, before you get to love and then to marry, there are many decisions to make along the road, such as when to have sex, safe sex, and the responsibility that comes with it.

I am not sure that nowadays young people understands the importance of safe sex...!

- I know, Dad. How safe is safe? Taking precautions is not being a coward, as Haitians say!

- You know, there is a choice to make, son. The right time and the right person. The best thing you can do is take your time before you ever get seriously involved with a girl.

- But you know, Dad, some girls sometimes think you're a wimp, if you don't pay attention to them... So you have to... you know... And, another guy might come along and take her away before you know it...

- Well, if the first guy that comes along takes her away from you, then she is certainly not the right one.

- Dad, did you ever regret marrying Mom?

- Regret? What a question! Your Mom and I were very much in love. I dated her for 4 years. Before leaving Haiti, I wanted her to know I was serious about our relationship. I was coming to the United States to build a future for us two, so, I married her before I left. I always knew she would be a good wife and she is. Your mother is a good mother too.

- I know. But Dad, haven't you met other women who seemed more interesting, you know what I mean…?

- Well... Men always meet women. And so do women. It's not whom you meet, it's whom you choose.

- Yup. But could you have had a mistress? I know Uncle...

- Steve, people make all kind of choices. There are different types of relationships between men and women. I know there are a lot of women out there. I am not blind but...

- Do you love Mom the same way you did when you first met her?

- That's an interesting question. I loved her when we met. I was crazy about her. She was crazy about me. Even though a long time has gone by, she is still lovely to my eyes. She is very special. She is so full of love and energy!

-True.

-Of course, people change physically, we all change somehow, for better or for worse. I have changed, she has changed. I have put on weight, I have a pot belly now and, because of heavy lifting at work, now, I have frequent backaches and other ailments. She, on the other hand, is getting grey hair. She talks a lot more and complains more often about this or that, but, you know, she is still lovely.

-Hmmm!

-I can still remember her candid little face when I first met her. She was only 14. She was only a child but I knew that later I would date her. Today, we are two inseparable lovers and friends; we have invested most of our love, our time, our energy, our health and assets together. We share our wonderful children.

- Dad, is it still the same love?

- The same, you bet. Now I am a man of experience and I am more secure. I enjoy being a man, son, and your mother is happier than ever. We are very much in love. We love each other. I am satisfied with my life.

- Aren't you bored with the same woman?

- Enough foolishness! No, *monchè*! Wait until you know what real love is. It's not comparable with some of the relationships you hear about nowadays.

- You know, Dad, I never thought that you and Mom could be so much in love. I thought love was only for younger people. I thought you two were old folks.

- I am young! You are younger but I am young! Haven't you seen Grandfather? Ask him, he will tell you he is the most seductive man you can meet. Of course he had a couple of flings but he is in love with your Grandmother.

- At 80 years old? He thinks he is seductive? He is really old, Dad! He must be faking!

- So what! Let him fake! That's part of life, man. Son, a man wants to be a man forever.

- You know, Dad, I would like to talk to you about a friend of mine. She is a real nice girl. We have spent some good times together in High School. She has been admitted to Cornell University. That doesn't mean I am serious about her but....

- I got your point. I get your point, son. I will enjoy meeting her.

- You know, Dad, you're cool.

- Really? What do you mean?

- Well, I mean, you are like a friend, just as close. You know, it's interesting to talk with you. I am getting to know you better... Dad, regarding school, don't worry, you'll be proud of me.

- I'm not worried. I know you will make it!

-You're cool, Dad!

Steve felt something special at the bottom of his heart after having this talk with his father. He thinks of some of his friends who say their fathers are like policemen behind them, always scolding, criticizing or pushing them away if not whipping them.

He looks at his father, the one they call TiJan, and feels himself very happy to have a father like that. It doesn't bother him anymore that his father has an accent and that his last name isn't as easy to pronounce as American last names. He realizes that Haitian parents have something special to appreciate and veneer. He knows his father is trying hard to adjust and adapt his values to the American way. He has heard his uncle Gaston talks about the way kids used to be whipped in Haiti... The way his grandparents were strict and stiff with his dad and siblings. He appreciates his father's patience and kindness.

He realizes the dilemma of some Haitian parents to reconcile the way they were brought up with the new way. He thinks his Dad is cool. He is a real model for him. Now, they are like friends.

He is so glad that he has always taken school seriously. He remembers how his mother used to come home from work and check his homework when he was in elementary school. He remembers how his father used to make him read two hours every night. He remembers how tired he used to be, falling asleep on the sofa, next to him. He looks now at his father and he knows what is expected from him. Success is the motto.

No, there is no room for failure!

Steve feels himself getting older. He is becoming a man. He is taking the road to college seriously. He knows where he is going and he knows how to get there. He shakes his head and smiles as he repeats:

-You're cool, Dad.

Nobody knows what is going on in this young man's head. Such a loving young man. A long silence follows. Both, father and son looks in the same direction. The road to success.

# CHAPTER 7

## An Old Sugar Bag - The Family is Reunited

Steve has completely recovered. His mother and father had a long conversation with him to help him understand how he needed to act in order to avoid trouble in the future. You know young men nowadays need to be kept on a leash in order for you to be able to protect them.

According to the latest news, Jera, the last of the Bonplezi family still remaining in Haiti, finally got on a little flimsy boat with his wife Edit and their six children. That's what Maman Plezi and Papa Sonson, the old folks, said on the telephone. But since then, no one has gotten any news. Gaston had a bad dream. Since then, he can't stop thinking of what might have happened to them. In his dream, Anit, Jera's eldest, had come to tell him that the boat had sunk. Two days later, there was still no news... Now, we are in Miami at the home of Gaston...

The telephone is ringing. Gaston doesn't know who is on the line and the person doesn't know him. It's a stranger.

Ring... ring... ring.

The stranger talks emotionally. "Hello, is this the home of Gaston Bonplezi?"

Gaston replies in a firm but broken voice. This is Gaston Bonplezi. Who is calling please?

- You don't know me, says the stranger. They call me Tifrè. Somebody gave me a message for you. Are you Gaston Bonplezi?

- Of course. Didn't I just tell you!

- Well, it's a guy named Jera who gave me a message to give you. He told me to tell you he is at Guantanamo Base with his wife and children. Do your best to get them out of there!

- Where are you calling from?

- Well… I don't know. I don't know any place at all in this country. I am staying with somebody, he told me not to tell anyone where I am...

- Where did you see Jera, did you come on the same boat as he did?

- Yes, I didn't know him before that but now he looks almost out of his mind. Is he a person who talks to himself constantly?

- Jera Bonplezi, you mean?

- Yes, of course. He is the one I am talking about. I don't know the wife. He didn't tell me any of his business. The only thing I know is that he told me to tell you to do something to get him out of there. The only way he and his family can come into the US is if they say they are refugees, otherwise they'll be sent back to Haiti.

- How was the trip?

- Don't even talk about it! An American boat came to save us. We were 100 on the boat, only 34 of us survived!

- What? Are they all safe, husband, wife and children?

- I don't know how many of them there were but there were some kids among those that drowned.

- God, you are killing me!

- You shouldn't have asked me, my friend...

- Please give me the telephone number you are calling from.

- What, are you crazy? I have to go... I am stealing now by calling you, this call is going on these people's bill...

The stranger hangs up. Gaston gets up, he picks up the phone again, to call TiJan's home. He speaks to TiJan and tells him the story he heard from the stranger. TiJan gives him Paul's number at the hospital. The two brothers meet right away and together they go off to see how they can get Jera released...

Two days after the anonymous stranger had called to tell Gaston that Jera was in Guantanamo, Gaston spoke with a Catholic priest who told him not to worry, that in a week he was going to get Jera and his family over here. The family had become extraordinarily distraught. Everybody forgot about themselves, they could only concentrate on Jera's situation. People aren't even talking about Steve at all. Steve at this moment is talking to a girl on the phone. He is trying to make an impression on her while she tries to keep at bay.

- Would you be interested in going for a movie tonight?

- Well, I am not sure. I haven't finished my homework and besides, I think I'll rather not.

- Why? Are you interested in someone else?

- Am I supposed to tell you everything?

- Sure! I want to know everything. Am I not your sweetheart?

- Listen, Steve, Sheila tells me you have been giving her the same story.

- Not true. She is jealous.

Heidi, the young woman, is not interested in letting Steve catch her, so she decides to change the subject but Steve is too smart for her.

- How have you been since your operation?

- Fine, I need someone sweet.

- Steve, I have to go.

As for Tika, she is breathless, she prays the whole day long. She prays to Saint Jude each time she hears the clock's chime. But, since the loud crash she heard as she was praying to him recently, she doesn't mention Saint Jude's name any more. She has started a novena, she goes to charismatic prayer meetings, and she visits every church so that the priest Gaston spoke with can get Jera and his family out of Guantanamo. She has made room in the house for Jera and his family, she has prepared a room for them, Jera and Edit will come to live with them. She already foresees how they all will live together. She undertakes a major housecleaning, cleaning every corner...

You have heard Tika say that the relatives you bring over or those you take in become the whip that beats on you but she would never let her relatives go knock on a stranger's door. Tika loves her family too much for that.

She hears a key turning in the lock of the door, she runs to open it. It's TiJan. She sees from the looks of him that there is no news. She has to ask him anyway. You never know...

- Jan, no news yet?

- No news yet... I am not living... I am dying inside...This thing is killing me. What is happening to us, my God!

- Come and have a bowl of beef feet stew.

- I don't want anything. I can't eat. My heart is tight; I'll eat when I get news of Jera.

- Do you think I should call the family in New York and those in Chicago?

- There's only one person I want you to call and that's Solanges. That's important.

While Tika is trying to get through to talk to Solanges who lives in Canada, TiJan realizes that there has been a major housecleaning in the house. He has a secret place in the house where he hides a little money. Not much. Some money he has been putting away for Steve's schooling. He notices Tika has been in the place where he hides the money. His heart jumps.

- Carmène, Carmène, where are you?

- I'm on the telephone. I am calling Solanges.

- Get off the phone this minute and come here, what were you doing in my things?

- What things? I didn't touch anything.

- Haven't I told you to never go into those boxes, those over there I mean!

- I didn't touch any box of yours, the only thing I did was to throw away a few empty boxes that were in the way...

- Throw them away? Where did you throw them away?

- In the dumpster, outside.

TiJan dashes off like a madman rushing to get to the trash. Tika goes running behind him to help him.

- Jan, what did you lose?

- *Machè*! Leave me alone! You can go inside...You threw out something of mine that is important.

- But, what is it? It has to be something awfully small, if I didn't even see it. How big is it?

- Go inside, please, go inside! Call Steve for me. Tell him to stay off the telephone; I'm waiting for a call.

Carmen goes to call Steve who has to get off the phone. He is constantly on the phone flirting with young women. He is going through that stage. He goes to help his father. He is amazed to see his father with three quarters of his body inside the dumpster, pulling out bags of trash.

- What is it, dad? What are you looking for?

- Please, just help me. When you find it, you will know.

- Is it something big or small? Give me some kind of description, please.

- I don't like nosey children!

- Come on, dad, how can I help you if I don't even know what I am supposed to be looking for. I really want to help you. I really do.

- I am looking for a dirty and wrinkled brown bag, about the size of a cantaloupe, a sugar bag that's about the size of a coconut.

- Why would you want a dirty wrinkled bag for?

- That's my business!

- Dad, when are you going to stop treating me as if I was a child...I am eighteen! We should be able to talk to each other as friends do, don't you think?

- Well, okay, it's no time to be arguing. Besides, I am very nervous about the bag. It's very important. We must find it!

- What is in there, dad, some kind of treasure?

- Son, don't make a joke of this! My whole savings are in there!

- What do you mean?

- It's...well...it's... money...!

- What? Why did you keep your money in that bag for?

- Shut up! Shut your mouth!

- Dad, my God, how could you do something like that? I thought you were wiser than that! Anybody, but anybody, could have thrown it away, come on, Dad! How could you do such a mindless thing!

- Because I am saving money for you, for your college expenses. That's your school money.

- But, God! Dad, you're supposed to keep money in the bank, not in an old dirty wrinkled bag! Now, what are we going to do!

- Just keep looking, look for the bag...

Many minutes have already elapsed. TiJan and Steve have turned the whole dumpster upside down, opened every trash bag. Steve is upset because he still can't understand how such an intelligent person as his father could hide the money at home in a little bag! What does his father think banks are for! They look through everything; they open so many trash bags, becoming intimately familiar with everybody's trash, with everything the neighbors have eaten for the previous week. There is such a stench coming from it all, you have to apologize to your nose for the awful smell.

However, God is with them...

- Oh, here is a brown bag. Is this the one?

- My son! Oh God! How glad I am... Do you realize I have thousands of dollars in this bag!

- What! What! Dad, this is crazy, it makes no sense at all! You've got to take it to the bank immediately! It's not safe keeping that much money at home...A burglar...

- Don't say that! I would have died if that had happened. Okay, I will take it to the bank. Listen. When we get back to the house, you don't have to tell your mother everything we just talked about. She doesn't have to know everything. You know your mother. Let her keep praying.

They go back to their house. They find Tika waiting for them, very much afraid.

- Did you find it?

- Huh Huh!  Don't worry. We got it.

- Oh, thank you, God! Thank you, Saint Jude! Well, where did you find it exactly?

- Don't worry about it.

- But I have to know what it is so I don't throw it out again!

- You don't have to worry about it. You won't see it anymore.  You won't be throwing it away… Anyway, I see you did great work in the house. I see you have gotten things ready for the folks who are arriving. Now we have to find out when they are coming, or even, if they are coming.

- They will come, the way my sole is itching me I know there got to be some important news on the way. Wait and see. If they don't arrive today then some unexpected money will be coming into the house. Wait and see…

If Tika had known the money had come back into the house in that little bag, then she would have understood what was making her foot itch like that!

TiJan now goes into his room for a little rest. He is going to think about how he nearly lost five thousand dollars. He realizes that Steve's idea of putting the money in the bank is a good one but he wonders if they will believe him when he says he saved up the money working at a part time job for so many years.

Tika is by her son's side wondering why Jan didn't want to tell her what he had lost. She thinks it must have been some important document. She puts the thought away in the back of her mind. She has too many important things to think about, she can't waste her time thinking about a dirty brown bag!

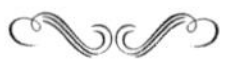

The telephone is ringing. Steve rushes to get it; he thinks it's one of his girlfriend's calls, but not so. It's..............Jera!

- Is it Uncle Jera, the one in Guantanamo? He tells himself.

Steve's heart starts pounding heavily. He knows that when his uncle arrives, it's going to be a big event for the family. Let's hear what is happening...

Ring................ring...............ring.

- Bonplezi's residence... Yes, this is Steve. Are you Uncle Gerard? Are you un- cle Je - ra?

- Yes, I am your Uncle Jera. Where's your father?

- He is here.... Are you coming here, I mean, are you arriving here today?

- For sure. Where is your father? Call him for me.

- Okay, I will call him for you... Dad, would you pick up the phone please. It's Uncle Gerard.

It's impossible to describe how TiJan felt, how his heart was pounding in his chest. We can't describe how his eyes filled with water; how he rushed to the phone for the moment he was waiting for...

- Hello. Jera?

- Yes, brother, *Se* Jera. We have arrived. We are in Miami now. That Father Bataille is a good guy. He got us here finally... How are you? How are the children? Where is Tika?

- Tika is here with us. She has been getting the house ready for your arrival since the last three weeks. She is anxiously waiting for you all to get here… Where are you exactly...? Give me the address so I can come to pick up you all.

- *Monchè*, let me have you talk with somebody who can give you directions; I don't know anything yet about this country.

A woman's voice comes on the telephone:

- Hello, what is it? What part of Miami are you in?

- I am in the Southwestern area. I will be taking US-I.

- I am the one to tell you how to get here. How can you be telling me what highway you will be taking? Do you know where you are coming to?

- There is nothing for me not to understand. Aren't you calling from Little Haiti?

- That's right. To come here, you are going to take Miami Street. When you get to Second Avenue you will take a right down the street, then when you get to the end and you go down until you don't know where you are, come upon Eighteenth Street and then, you will turn again...

- What kind of strange directions are those? *Machè*, please excuse me, but, that's not a way to give directions! What is it that turns and goes down? And how do I know what road is going up or down? Those are not cardinal directions! said TiJan, impatiently.

- Well, that's the way I can explain it. Whenever I give directions, people always get here without a problem! You can't be any more stupid than anybody else!

- *Machè,* That's not what I am saying. You are not in Haiti any more. Here, there are maps. Get one, learn how to use it. Maps will show you all the streets in every area. If you know where you are going, you can look at the map and understand how to go where you're going. Anyway, only give me your address. You don't have to give me directions. I can come to your place!

What a strange person!

TiJan, Tika and Steve hit the road. They are on their way to meet Jera, Edit and the children. They found the address without any problem. When they arrive, Jera was standing outside waiting for them. In the meanwhile, Gaston has also arrived. Oh, it should be a celebration. They hug Jera. They hug him with tears in their eyes. Jera is just the shadow of himself. He isn't himself any more. He has lost about fifty pounds. He is not the Jera we knew! It's just his bones and skin that have come here. His eyes are pulled back, his skin drawn. He looks transfigured.

- Here is the one that was missing for our family to be whole! Here is the last of the Bonplezi in the United States. *Monchè*, I feel as though I am dreaming. This is my brother! This is my brother!

- It's not a joke! Oh look... Is that Steve? This is Steve, isn't he? He is so grown up, isn't he? He is already a man! He is a tall young man. Oh, look at Tika, my God, come to me, Tika. Jera is so emotional.

- My old brother, come to me! Where have you been, brother! That time has come for our family to be reunited! Where is Edit?

Tika walks into the host's house and she runs to see Edit.

- Edit, it's you, my sister? Where have you been?

- Her I am… Here I am now. We are here....

- Where are the children?

That's the question...

Edit had to tell them about the voyage. The boat voyage…. The boat had sunken, children and adults had fallen in the water, and some people had drowned. Three, not one, but three of their children were among those who didn't make it. Yes, Oh Eternal one, Saint Jude, why did you do this to us!

Let us leave the family alone as they grieve.

# CHAPTER 8

## Miracle after Miracle

Jera and Edit arrived two days ago. They are staying with TiJan and Tika. Even though Tika had said she would not put up family members any more. When the time came, she was the first one to open her door to let them in. She had cleaned the house, emptied a room to give them, even before they had arrived. She is amazed to see how Jera's children have grown. How beautiful they are, how beautiful indeed!

There is one cause for enormous sadness. The shipwreck Jera, Edit and the children had been through! When Jera was relating how the sea had become so rough, how some people were throwing themselves into the ocean, it made all of them tremble. Jera told the story with such deep sadness that everybody's stomach was turned upside down. The hardest thing to have to listen to was when he said that some people were throwing others off the boat because of the overcrowding. That's how Anit, the younger sister and Junior fell into the ocean. You can imagine how it felt for the parents? No, it is not possible even to imagine.

You cannot imagine it!

This was what Gaston's dream was about!

When she got to Guantanamo, Edit was unable to speak for several days, as if she had been aphasic. She spent a few days without being able to utter a single word... She was like a crazy woman. She spent her nights at the camp roaming around, as if she was going to find the children, as if they had lost their way and she had to look for them, as if they would be returning soon. They did not return!

The whole family is now together, at least, everybody from Tika's house and from Paul's house too. Gaston and Margaret are there too. After Jera had given them the news, nobody knew what to say, they could only put their hands to their mouths. There was a long silence. Edit and Jera looked as if they would never be the same as before. However, all the children were already playing together, as if they all had been together for a long time. It seemed that some kind of transition was beginning to take place.

As I was speaking with you, visitors have come and gone. A lot of people have come to greet the family at TiJan's place. Some come to offer their condolences, but have no idea what to say: three children all at once taken away by Simbi... What can you say! What could you possibly say to console the parents and the family!

You just can't. There is no way.

My God, what is all this!

Some people come to see Edit and Jera's faces, to see what they can read on them, what traces Haiti has left on their appearances, what the hope of coming here has done to them. Some come to pick up the gossip, you know, about the Bonplezi family! I was there too; I went there to get the whole story so I could tell it to you.

But, nobody can understand anything. Edit doesn't say a word. Not even a tear comes out of her eyes. She grabs her chin in her hands and thinks. She looks like a statue. You can't even tell by looking at her what she is thinking: she seems present but she isn't. Jera too seems heartbroken but he takes courage, he talks about one thing only: "I cannot yet understand anything here. This is so different here.... I don't know where to go to get a job or where to go to take the bus..." Jera seems not coherent,

Tika welcomes everyone that comes to the door. People never stop coming and going. The door is continually opening and closing. Tika makes lot of coffee; she serves lot of *patés*, meat patties, chicken patties, codfish patties, hot patties. Here she is entertaining... People come for the gossip. That's Miami. The grapevine is spreading the news all over: "Three Bonplezi kids drowned at sea. Do you think that maybe the parents did it? People's business is a mystery... They must have thrown the children into the sea to have their luck changed... The mother wouldn't be looking so strange if she wasn't guilty..."

Anyway, all the visitors are welcome.

The minister's wife came too:

- Well, I've heard they have arrived, Glory be to God! God knows what he is doing. Do you hear me, sister, keep the faith. Pray! He hears you and will give you strength.

- Thank you, replies Edit, how are you?

- Well, I am here. I should be asking you how you are.

- Well, we're not too bad, answers Edit.

- I tell her, says Tika, she needs to get some rest, take her time. No reason to hurry. She can wait about a month before she goes looking for work.

- We'll look for you in our church, sister, adds the minister's wife. Wednesday, all of us from the women's choir will come and pray with you.

People continue coming and going.

Knock.............knock...............knock.

"The door's open, come in. Who is it?" calls out Tika.

Two Jehovah's Witnesses appear at the door. Everybody from every religion wants to give the Bonplezi family courage. Faith is free; you can get it for nothing.

"We are students of the Bible, say the Jehovah's Witnesses. We have come to visit you and share a message from the Bible with you because *the Kingdom of Jehovah is near!"*

The pastor's wife chides them with authority: "We don't invite Jehovah's Witnesses to come here. We have no time for that, you had better move on."

Tika feels offended: "Madam Pastor, besides the fact that you are putting people out of my house, let me tell you that my home is God's house. Whether visitors are Catholic, Protestant, Jehovah's Witness or Voodooists, if they come to pray, they're going to pray, as long as it's God's words they bring. I have no problem with anybody…"

- But, sister, you cannot serve God in voodoo!

- They are all calling upon God. I am not the one separating them all, as long as they are calling upon God, as long as they are talking about love for one's neighbor and love for life, then I have no objection. I have nothing to say against them.

- That's not the way to have faith, what do you say, sister Edith?

- I can't see it like that. Especially after the experience I have just lived through, I've come to have another definition of life that goes beyond religion. It's in difficult moments that you can grasp the meaning of life...

- Oh, I thought you were a Christian but I see you are a heretic.

- Well, I find that you are attacking me without reason. I have to tell you...

- I don't want anybody upsetting my wife, intervenes Jera. Edit, let's go into your room. Stay inside. You need to rest.

- But we should take time out to thank God for the huge blessing he has bestowed upon us. Arriving as you have in the United States, in the condition you did, is a big blessing. You need to give God praise in church. We are having a service at church on Sunday.

- It's not about going to a service, one of the Jehovah's Witness interjects; it's about the end of this world that is near. The Kingdom is at hand.

- Well, you know, interrupts Tika, leave the poor family in peace, you hear. Let them find their way on their own. When they start looking for a church to go to, or a temple, if that's what they want, they will decide!

And Tika asks everyone to leave.

A lady arrives at the door, it's a woman dressed in black, with a girl about twelve years of age. She says:

- Is it here Ms. Edit lives?

- Yes, this is Mrs. Jeras's home. Edit, there's someone for you, Tika calls out to Edit.

- Oh, it's little Ketli! How are you doing, dear?

- I'm okay, Ms. Edit, I came to see you because I miss you a lot. I always remembered you.

- Ketli had told me, says the lady in black, that you acted always like a mother to her in Haiti. That little girl speaks so much about you. I did my best to get the afternoon off so she could come and see you.

- I am so touched and pleased, what grade are you in now?

- I'm in ninth grade now.

- Tell Ms. Edit how well you are doing in school.

- Oh really, you are doing well?

- Yes, I am. Everything you taught me is what they're teaching me now. I am doing well. They've put me in a special program now.

- That's wonderful. You left Haiti just about a year ago. That means education in Haiti must be pretty good.

- It must have some good aspects, says the lady in black, because it seems that the kids adapt very quickly here when they come. Maybe they are lacking certain practical aspects but the good discipline in Haitian schools helps the children when they get here. She is in what they call a Magnet School. Ms. Edit, are you going to continue to teach school here?

- I don't know yet, I haven't found work yet, I'll take whatever I get.

- Where I work they need help but I don't know if it's the type of job you want.

- I don't care what it is, I'll take whatever I can find. I have to start somewhere.

- Well, I work in a shrimp factory.

- Really? I'm interested.

- Hmmm. Sure?

-Why not? Work is work.

- Not quite because peeling shrimps is hard work.

- What is it that you do at work?

- First, you have to go and get the shrimps in the cold room, after that, you clean them, you wash them, you remove their heads and intestines and then you pack them.

- My, my, that seems like an easy job.

- Well, if you would like, I'll introduce you, I'll come and get you Monday morning.

- Oh, that will make me so happy. I'll appreciate that a lot really... Jera, do you hear, I may already have a job... Tika, what do you think?

- Well, I don't know about that, replies Tika. You are the one who is so much in a hurry to go to work. You could wait, you know. You would get something else. Aren't you comfortable with us here? No rush, I say… Anyway, I will pray, you hear, I am going to pray to Saint Jude for you, he will decide what is good for you... Anyway, Edit, tomorrow, I won't be here. Edit, please make yourself at home. Whatever you find in the refrigerator is yours to cook. I went food shopping for you; there are all kinds of food in the fridge. Cook the food you like. Do just as you would have done at your own home.

Night time comes, everybody goes to bed. Edit spends the whole night long without shutting an eye. She still hasn't gotten over it. She can't get used to this country either. She can't accept the fact that she left Haiti with six children and arrived here with only three. She doesn't shut an eye. Early in the morning, from her bed, she hears Tika getting up. She hears TiJan getting up; she hears everything that's going on in the house.

It's now Sunday morning, at nine o'clock. Edit and Jera are alone in the house with the children. Tika has gone out, TiJan is at work.

- Jera, do you want to eat something?

- No, I'm not hungry. No, I am going to sit by the phone and make a few calls to see if I can find a job. I also want to go around the city… I'm giving myself a week to find a job.

- Let me make some coffee. Tika told me to cook some food. I looked in the freezer and found a turkey. I put it to soak so it would defrost.

- Well, do you know how to cook a turkey? In Haiti, it was the maid that cooked for us but here there is no maid….

- You know, I can't find where Tika keeps her sour oranges and lemons, I don't see where she stores chives, or garlic or anything... Here's your coffee.

- The coffee is good. I'll have a piece of bread and some butter with it.

- Well, Jera, get up and get your food, there's no maid here, you know.

- *Madam*, you don't have to worry, we are not going to be here for long, and everything will be fine. We will have our own place soon. Give me a chance and soon you'll see.

- I have no problem here to be in this house… I was ready for all this. I was ready for anything, except my children...

- *Madam*, come here and let me talk to you. Come here and let me say something to you in your ear.

- You have nothing to tell me. Let's put that matter away.

- I know it's my fault.

- Don't say that. I didn't say that. I'm just going through tough times now. I know that everything will fall back into place one day... One day! But now…

- I'm here for you, Edit. One will watch over the other, isn't that right?

- Yes, *monchè.* One will watch over the other. Well, let me go and see if the turkey has begun to defrost. It's been in water since early this morning.

Edit gets up, she uncovers the pot she had put the turkey in and what does she see! Speechless at first, she yells out suddenly.

- What am I seeing! What is this? She screams.

- What is it, what's happening? What's in there? Replies Jera.

Jera gets up from where he was sitting to go and see why Edit has cried out so loudly.

- Come and see, Jera, come quickly, come and see.

- Oh, what is that! What is that! The pot is full of money! Mezanmi...!

But when he comes and looks at what it is, he too is startled. He didn't just yell, he exploded and went crazy.

The pot, let me tell you, a big one, is full, with the turkey and the water to the very edge. Now it looks like dollar soup, you can't even see the turkey. It's now a *dollar consomme*, completely green with greenbacks right before their eyes! What kind of magical turkey is that! Three days after arriving in Miami! They are speechless! Look at that pot full of money! And not just any dollar bills! Fifty and one hundred dollar bills only.

Jera and Edith are happy and frightened at the same time. What a miracle! They are afraid to put their hands into the water to check if the whole pot is filled with money, to check if the turkey was transformed into dollars or if the turkey is still in the bottom of the pot.

- Look at that dollar soup!

- God, that's strange. What does that mean? And, there's nobody home.

- There is nobody home...

- Jera, this frightens me. This is not normal. Where are Jan and Carmène now? What should we do?

- What should we do? The miracle is not happening to them! It happens to us!

- I have never seen anything like that in my life before. What are we going to do? Should I put my hands into the water?

- Of course, let's do it quick, get the money out, I am going to get a suitcase to put it into quickly.

- Jera, you put your hands in the put. Not me… I don't feel comfortable doing it.

- Oh, aren't you funny? You would rather go and work in the shrimp factory tomorrow than go and open an account in the bank!

- Jera, there's something funny in this. What if the money is not supposed to be for us?

- Then it wouldn't have happened in the pot. Do it quickly, put your hands in the water; put the money on the towel over there while I dry each bill. Then, we'll put them all in the pillowcase.

As the two are thinking about the miracle that has just happened to them, while they are drying the bills and putting them into the pillow case, a key is heard in the lock. Tika appears on the scene. She comes upon the two of them while they are in full action.

- Oh, why are you wetting your money like that? What are you doing? Besides they're big bills, you should go put them in the bank early tomorrow morning!

- Yes, replies Edit, that's what we're thinking of. We haven't decided yet what to do.

Edit does not want to keep the secret. The whole thing is too much for her. She wants to tell Tika all about it.

- You shouldn't have come with all that money, advises Tika. You could have been killed.... for it.

Now is Jera's turn not to keep the miracle to himself. They both drop all their secret plans. They see Tika so innocent and kind, there's no way they can lie to her.

- Tika, says Jera, we didn't come here with the money. We found it in the pot.

- What? In what pot? Let me see. How could that happen? That's a miracle for you! That's Saint Jude's doing, and God the Father's too.

- Remember, you told me to cook, didn't you, asks Edit? I looked in the freezer and saw a turkey. I took it out. I put it to soak in water so it could defrost and when I came back to check on it, I took the cover off the pot, and, instead of the turkey, all I see is money.

- Oh, Mezanmi, Mezanmi, Saint Jude, it's a miracle. It's my dream! That explains my dream...Last night, while I was asleep I dreamt it was raining, it was raining, I tell you it was raining a lot. In my sleep, I could see the water spreading everywhere, all the furniture in the house was wet, everybody was wet but you Edit and you too Jera, you were the only ones who weren't. You were completely dry. Your feet were completely dry. Yes, it is the dream.

... My God, what miracle is that, what should we do? God the Father, enlighten us, make us aware of the mission you have for us. What do you want us to do? Saint Jude, my patron...

- As for me, comments Jera, I think we should finish drying the bills and put them in the pillow case. Then, we can count them to find out how much money there is. We have to go buy you a turkey too, Tika. We have you give you your turkey back…

- Wait a minute, says Edit to Jera, let's first of all understand what's happening. Let's take our time before we make any decision.

- Well, exclaims Jera, the money can't stay here overnight. We have to have a plan of action. First of all, where to put the money tonight...

- Well, suggests Tika, in this house, TiJan is the one who handles all the money, let's wait until he comes home, or let me call him. He doesn't like me to call him at work but this is for a serious matter.

Tika goes to the telephone and calls TiJan. Tika is overcome. My God, what a miracle! That's Saint Jude's doing for sure, for sure... He's a saint who really understands. He sees this couple who just arrived is in financial need. Look at that miracle! Look at that, look at that!

Ring..................ring.....................ring.

- Hello Jan, she says nervously, it's Tika. Can I speak with you for a minute?

- Huh, what's the matter?

- Something has happened...a miracle.

- What kind of miracle is it?

- Well, Edit was going to cook a turkey….

- What turkey?

- There aren't two or three turkeys here!

- What? Don't tell me you took the turkey from the freezer?

- I wasn't thinking, and, it's not Edit's fault. I told her to cook what she wanted.

- I'm coming home right now. Stay with them. I'll be right there. Tell them I'm coming right home.

- What's the matter? Well... Okay... I'll wait for you...

Tika hangs up the telephone.

# CHAPTER 9

## Surprise after Surprise

A miracle happened at Tika's house. It was after defrosting a turkey that Edit and Jera got their first shock in Miami: a turkey transformed into dollars. At least that's what they thought. Tika, Edit and Jera were all shouting miracle. Now, TiJan is on his way home, he is coming to see the miracle.

- I called TiJan at his job, comments Tika, I spoke to him, and he is coming home now.

- You didn't have to disturb him at work for that, protests Jera. I don't see any need for it. He was going to come home later anyway, wasn't he?

- My God, it really startled Jan because he is leaving his job, he is rushing home. He is really shocked.

- Tika, asks Edit, could you make me a strong cup of coffee, please?

- I'll have some too, continues Jera. A big cup. It's a real big miracle that's going to change all our plans, *madanm*.

Not even ten minutes had passed, the coffee wasn't even ready yet, TiJan was already home. It seems as if he flew, he flew back home. The matter is serious.

Do you remember the money he had hidden in the brown bag that Tika had thrown away without realizing it? Well, TiJan still had the money at home. He rolled the money up real tight, and he put it inside a turkey. The whole five thousand dollars! And then he put the turkey into the freezer! And he told everybody not to ever touch that turkey, that's all. You remember it was money he was saving to pay for Steve's college. Poor dad! It seems as if that secret will kill him one day. He had been saving that money for a long time. This is his saved earnings from a past part time job. He had been putting that money away one hundred dollars at the time. Over time the money had grown and was now quite a big sum. Now, those people came and... By thunder, it's a real curse! He arrives like a madman.

- Where's Carmène? Wait a minute, here. Jera and Edit, I need to speak with you.

- I'm so happy you came, Edit says to him. You can advise us in this matter.

- Look TiJan, his wife tells him, it's a miracle, It's Saint Jude's doing.

- Be quiet, Tika, What do you know. It's no miracle, and it's no doing of Saint Jude's. It's some money a friend of mine asked me to keep for him.

- Oh God, Jera groans disappointingly, what are you saying, brother?

- Brother, I am not in a joking mood.  Didn't that money come from inside the turkey that was in the freezer?

TiJan sticks his arm in the pot without pulling up the long sleeve of the white shirt he is wearing. He pulls the turkey out of the water and sticks his hand inside it. More money comes out…. TiJan tells Jera, Edith and Tika that someone entrusted him to keep the money safely for a major purpose. Since that is a big responsibility, he didn't want to put it somewhere where burglars could have gotten their hands on it...So he stocked it inside the turkey.

Shock, disappointment and silence ensued. Everybody is regretting that the miracle had aborted.

There was great sadness in Jera and Edit. They had imagined it was a miracle that was going to change their lives, and, coming to find out, it was just an April fool trick! TiJan took the pillow case and all the rest of the money that had remained inside the turkey. He dried all the bills. He counted them, bill by bill, until all of the five thousand dollars had been counted up. All the bills were there; there was not one missing.

However, TiJan is uncomfortable. Tika is silent. She doesn't say a word, she doesn't understand what happened. How was it possible that there was five thousand dollars in her house without her knowing about it? And in her own kitchen! In her own refrigerator! How could TiJan keep such a huge secret from her! What was she then in the household if he could keep such a secret from her!

Jera and Edit go into their room. They are as cold as ice. Tika too goes into her room to lie down. TiJan remains in the kitchen thinking. Steve had told him so. He decides to go into the bedroom to speak to Tika.

- How many more secrets do you keep from me? asks Tika.

- Tika, it's not a secret, I want to explain to you, listen to me. I made a serious mistake. A very serious mistake. I should never have put the money in the turkey.

- You see that too! Every day I open the refrigerator. I open it at least twenty times a day. Every day the money is looking at me and I am looking at it too! What do you have to say to me, huh?

- I didn't do it with bad intentions, Tika. Put yourself in my place. I didn't want to put the money just anywhere, in the event a burglar came. I always kept it to myself but I think now I should have told you about it. That was a big mistake. That was the biggest mistake.

- You understand that now, TiJan?

- You're right, *cheri*. You have plenty of reason to be mad at your husband.

- Then, why didn't you ever talk to me about the money? Even though it's not yours, you know that if you had lost it, I would have had to help you pay it back.

- *Cheri*, you are right, I'm telling you, you are right. Your husband made a big mistake, and he is the first one to acknowledge it. But, sweetheart, listen to me, listen carefully and keep your voice down, don't say a word... The money is ours!

- Mercy! Tika yells out as if a bomb had just exploded. You said what? What did you say, huh?

- Didn't I just tell you not to shout? It has been my dream to save money for Steve.

- Money for Steve, what money for Steve?

- The money for Harvard, don't you know? Even if he gets a scholarship, he will still need money for other little expenses. It is always an obsession of mine to be able to provide to him whatever he needs to go to college.

- I thought the money wasn't yours?

- My dear, please do not talk loud. The money is ours.

Tika screams once again. She hears the information but her mind cannot assimilate it! It is like a nightmare with a happy ending!

- What? I still don't understand. What? How come?

- Be quiet. Do not talk loud. You don't have to tell everyone our business. People might think we're rich.

- What are you saying, the money is ours? Well, why did you hide it in the turkey?

- *Machè*, this is how it happened. Do you remember when I was working in Gonzalez's office? Well, he used to pay me cash. I always put that money away, but...not in the bank.

- *Monchè*, you should have put it in the bank.

- *Machè*, I had just gotten in this country then, I didn't understand everything. At one time, I had gone to the bank and they asked me for identification, something like that, so I panicked. It took me time to come to the realization that one shouldn't wait till you have too much cash on hand before going to the bank. The teller might suspect you of wrong doing and call the police. They can imagine all kinds of things about you and where the money comes from.

- And what about me? How come I was never in the secret, huh?

- I don't know. I can tell you that very frankly, from my heart, I have no excuse, Tika. I must have thought that if you had known about the money, maybe you would have wanted to change our furniture or buy some jewelry. I don't know… I have no excuse!

- That's what you think about me?

- No, *machè*, I didn't think anything bad about you, I am not even sure there would have been any reason for me to think like that...

- Anyway, a surprise for a surprise. I have a surprise too, But, I am not speaking! And, it's a SURPRISE!

Meanwhile Edit and Jera had remained in their room. They dressed their children so they could go out for a while. It is something to have a miracle happen to you and then see it vanished in thin air just like that! Edit was so happy about the possibility of a miracle. Jera had felt it was a great opportunity to have starting money. Their children didn't even know anything about the whole matter; they had been watching television with Tika's children. The program had absorbed them so much that none of them had been aware of what had happened!

Anyway, it's okay, it was just a mirage. They go out for a walk. Outside, they look at everything their eyes come upon. They're interested in everything they see.

- So, Jera, that's what America is like!

- Yes, *machè*, we have come to a developed country, to the land of opportunities!

- What plans do you have? What do you see for us here in this strange country?

- I see we will both have a job. We will educate our children. And, I'll make you happy. I'll help at home; I'll learn to wash dishes, I'll cook, wash clothes, do some ironing, whatever is needed. In the meantime, I would like to go somewhere to meet other Haitians. We have to leave TiJan's house after no more than a month's time. What do you say about that?

- I don't see clearly yet. I don't understand how I got here, how I was able to get on that boat and come here, how I could have lost my children. One thing I know though, I am not here for nothing. I have to do something, so that my children's death will have not been in vain. I have to leave my mark in this world. I have to justify the sacrifice I made to embark in this journey and lose three children!

- Do you still love me, Edit?

- Why that question? Our love is not in danger. It's our mental status that's at risk. Starting today, there will have to be a reason for everything I do. There's going to be a reason for everything I do or don't do... Did you read the paper today?

- I didn't read it. You know, I don't understand English very well.

- I'm not too good at it either. However, from what I understand, the situation of Haitians in Miami is not too good.

- In what sense, you mean? They can't find jobs?

- There are problems at work, problems in the schools, social and economic problems. It seems to be a tough place to be in!

- Well, in our country, we were teachers. You know teachers have a mission. We'll pursue our mission.

- Yes, we will pursue our mission...

While Edit and Jera are taking stock of their situation and that of Haitians in Florida, Gaston is living another drama. He has just left a meeting, and he is getting home. His house is as spotless as on New Year's Day. As soon as he is home, he notices something is different. Everything is in its place; the kitchen smells good, as if something good is cooking. He looks everywhere but doesn't see Margaret. Oh, it seems she is not home?

Meanwhile Tika and TiJan continue their conversation. They heard Edit and Jera go out. That's quite natural to them. People have a right to go out and, after all, they are adults. Besides, Tika has something she needs to tell TiJan, just as he had kept a secret from her, she too, had her own secret and she is almost ready to tell him about it. And, he wants to hear about it right away:

- Well, what's the secret you've been keeping from me, Tika?

- Nothing. Didn't you just finish telling me about yours? Well, I have my secret too. It's my secret!

- Look, Tika, I am going to complain to Saint Jude about you! Talk fast; I need to know what's happening here that I'm not aware of!

- It's nothing, TiJan. Look, you're making too much of a big thing out of it!

- Tika, I'm giving you a minute, if you don't tell me what your secret is, I'm going to report you to Saint Jude.

- TiJan, stop joking! You are making fun of Saint Jude. You know he is a very good saint but he is touchy too!

- Well, what do you want me to do? I want to know your secret right away. Immediately!

While TiJan and Tika are having this conversation, about whose secret is being kept from whom, there is a telephone call being placed from New York to Miami. It's Nicole, Ms. Nicole from New York who is talking to her good friend and sister-in-law Sandra in Miami. Let's have a listen.

- Hello, Sandra, it's Nicole.

- Niki, *ma chère*, how are you?

- Well, I'm here. I'm calling to tell you about a double surprise. First, it seems that Margaret is preparing to pull a fast one on Gaston.

- What kind of trick?

- Well, you know she has been waiting a long time for him to make a move. And, you know he has been dragging his feet. He has never made any move whatsoever. Not even an engagement ring!

- I advised her to sack him. I don't see what she sees in him anyway. A woman like her, she has everything any big shot in Haiti would want in a wife. I know for a fact that my brother Boris would be interested in her.

- Hmmmm! Listen, my second surprise is that I'm coming to Florida for a short visit. You know I have so little time.

This is the first time I take a vacation in ten years. Too many bills, sweetheart!

- How many days will you be here?

- Listen. Hear my plans: I am coming for a week with the children. I am taking them to Disney World for a day. The rest of the time they will spend together with Tika's children.

- You mean you are not going to stay with me?

- Eh, eh, eh....Let me stay at Tika's. Those people will be so happy, so honored to have me, they'll prepare food, they'll take care of the children, and they'll take them out without my having to spend a penny. In the meantime, you and I we can go out and enjoy ourselves. You understand what I mean?

- Perfectly, my dear! I get it now. That's exactly what I used to do. Whenever I wanted to go on a second honeymoon, I would leave the children with Tika. But, I don't any more. The children have grown; I don't want *her* to be teaching them any bad manners.

- Yes, indeed. Has *she* taught them any bad manners?

- Of course, darling. *She* has a thing about Saint Jude. Can you imagine, little Ingrid came home one day wanting to pray to Saint Jude so he could help her find a violin she had lost! Another time, Sophie came home and told me she likes to chew on bones. I said to her: "When have you ever seen your mother or father do that?" She told me to ask Tika about it: "Ask Aunt Tika. She lets us do it. At her house, we chew on all the bones, right at the table!"

- Chewing on bones! Can you imagine that!

- Chewing on bones! For my children to see them chew on bones, to bite on bones, never! No, never! I don't let them go there anymore.

- To let the children chew on bones is terrible. But Sandra, if I have to pay a lot of money for babysitter, that might be even worse. You know, Sandra, I am not coming with a babysitter. That would be too expensive for me. I need to have a babysitter that doesn't cost anything. I think I'll have to let the children chew on bones for a week. It won't kill them, and besides, it'll be for free...As I told you, I am coming to witness Gaston's demise at Margaret's hands and I am coming to relax too. What's on your agenda?

- Well, there's going to be a banquet offered by the doctors' wives association in honor of a colleague from Finland.

- That sounds kind of nice.

- Indeed, there'll be only distinguished people there.

- Superb, I'll get a dress at Jarrod Boutique.

- Well, I too need to get something new after the problem I had with Paul.

- Which one? You two had problems?

- Oh, it was bad! We'll talk about it when you are here.

The two women continue talking about their plans. Nicole is getting ready to dump her children and all the work involved in taking care of them onto Tika while she is showing off at the physicians' wives party, arm and arm with her sister-in-law, *Madam* Sandra. That's something she really likes, so upon her return in New York, she can go back to her job and show what kind of people she was with. She will show off to anyone less off than her!

During all this time, Tika's has not yet revealed her secret.

- Well, are you going to tell me about your secret or not?

- Oh, it's nothing important. It's a little money I was putting away too. I don't have as much money as you, of course.

- Where is it? Where is it? Go and get it, Tika. Show it to me!

Tika gets up and goes to the dirty laundry basket. She pulls out an old pillow case. TiJan puts his hand to his head.

- What's that, Tika? Where are you going with that big bag?

- TiJan, don't shout. Stop making me feel like a fool. You aren't really seeing what you're thinking. It's not a lot of money. If the pillowcase looks big, it's because I've wrapped the money in several pillow cases.

That's how Tika was able to explain to TiJan that every week, she takes ten dollars from the food money, because, you never know, "just in case." However, she never has a chance to count the money. It is not that she is putting money away with the intention of doing anything with it in secret.

She never counts how much it amounts to. It might add up to a little sum. Who knows?

TiJan just listens to Tika without saying a word. Here is the person who had told him that he shouldn't keep money at home. This is also the same one who had gotten angry that he hadn't told her about the turkey!

TiJan and Tika are counting the money. Well, it's TiJan who opens the pillowcase. He opens ten others before he finally gets his hands on the money. It's a lot of small bills folded into minute sizes, like cigar rings which they start to unfold together. Let's start multiplying; Tika had been saving ten dollars a week for twenty years. How much money she has been saving?

- Tika, I just finished counting the money. I'm going to tell you how much there is. Well, I have just counted ten thousand four hundred dollars in that little bag of yours. Madam! MADANM! We have money for Steve's school. WOOYYYY!

- TiJan, you know you have just shocked me! All that money, you mean I was able to save all that money?

- Well, Tika, I told you, after so many years of hard work, you and I have earned the right to take a vacation.

- A vacation indeed? What will I do with the children?

- I think Nicole is coming to Florida soon; we can leave the children with her.

# CHAPTER 10

## From Arnold to Gaston

We have just learned how Tika and TiJan were able to accumulate a good sum of money. Without them having been aware of it, they now came to the realization they had fifteen thousand dollars, if not more. So, both TiJan and Tika had kept a secret from each other. However, all ended well, thanks be to the Lord. That's one of the reasons too they decided to take a vacation.

Meanwhile, don't forget that Nicole is planning to arrive during the same period. She doesn't even call Tika or TiJan to confirm her stay. She doesn't have money to spend on useless long distance calls. Nevertheless, she feels like calling Gaston. She has wanted to check on something for a long time. Rumor has it that Margaret is going to *R and R* (Revoke and Replace) Gaston. Anyway, even if Margaret is not planning to do it, Nicole wants to open her eyes. She knows someone in Haiti who would be very interested in Margaret. During that same period, Arnold, Nicole's husband, also plans to travel to Miami. This couple is quite strange; each spouse makes separate vacation plan.

In this chapter we will witness an event that is going to happen in Margaret's and Gaston's life. Sit back, relax and listen.

The phone is ringing at Gaston's place. It's Nicole calling Gaston for public relations purposes. However, Margaret answers the telephone. Just what Nicole wants!

- Hello, this is Margaret and Gaston's residence.

- Hi, Margaret, it's Nicole.

- Oh, Nicole, how are you? We're not too bad over here.

- I will be in Miami soon, so I decided to give Gaston a call... By the way, I am very surprised to find you at Gaston's. Rumor has it that you are revoking him.

- What does that mean?

- That you are going to break up with him.

- I don't understand, what do you mean *break up* with him? Say it in Creole, maybe I will understand better what you are saying. *Pale Kreyòl pou m ka konprann ou pi byen.*

- I mean you are going to leave him, no? You will *r and r* him. That you are going to end the relationship because he is not interested in marrying you.

- What? What are you talking about?

- Are you trying to make me think you're shocked?

- Of course, I am. Gaston and I are doing fine. We haven't *r-ed* nor will we *r*, there's not going to be any *r and r.*

- Well, so be it. Anyway, if you should ever be interested, I have a friend in Haiti who saw your picture...

- Gaston saw my picture first and he is the one I love. We can talk when you are here, don't waste your money talking about that, Nicole, you hear?

Nicole hangs up disappointed. She wonders how she will get Arnold's younger brother legally into this country. Margaret could have made that happen just like that.

While Nicole is trying to figure out another way she can bring Arnold's younger brother into the country, Arnold has been thinking about something else. Since he heard the news that Edit and Jera had left Haiti and arrived in Miami, he used that as an excuse to get out of the house. The relationship between Nicole and him is not sitting well, in a way, he feels like a free man. In fact, he feels like visiting an old girlfriend of his, someone he used to know in Queens and who has recently come to live in Miami. So, he parks his taxi in his carport and start polishing his best French hoping he will be highly seductive in Florida.

Upon his arrival, he makes his first stop at TiJan and Tika's house. He runs into Antoinette who happens to be in Miami for a brief halt after a stay in West Palm Beach. Antoinette is a sister-in-law he enjoys seeing. He cannot resist when he sees a beautiful woman. He just can't sit still. He has to start making passes. While everybody else is busy going back and forth around the house, Arnold recites poetry to Antoinette. He forgets who Antoinette is. Let's get a whiff of their conversation.

- Oh, *Madame*, what a pleasure to see you again. What an *enchantement.* Coquette as you are, just like a flower…

- Arnold, it cannot be any other way...

- I've always thought that Henry Claude hit the biggest jackpot marrying you. Nature has been so generous to you. Women like you should be kept in the museum of beauty so they can be admired. If I had a woman like you, I would feel like a prince.

- You are not a prince, Arnold. Don't dream too much, you can see me in magazines. You know I signed a contract with that company in Hollywood. *Mon cher*, success is pursuing me. I am no longer the little Antoinette you used to know.

- But you are the Antoinette I admire. I love successful women. They have the intensity of fire and the appeal of the forbidden fruit. They have always fascinated me.

- And they can drive you crazy too! Listen *mon cher*, don't fool yourself. You can't afford to have a successful woman! Not by driving a taxi in New York City anyway!

- Let me tell you, *dearest*, I am the happiest man in the world. I am a happy and free man.

- Frrreeee, aren't you married to my sister Nicole? Don't you have three children? Listen, *mon cherr*, in this world, you have to make choices. I have chosen the seduction of luxury, the tango of challenge. I like being important, I like to make a difference. I like the fairylike and comfortable aspect of wealth and glory. I could never imagine you being happy driving a taxi and much less so in New York City! Come on!

- Yes, happy, even in New York! Even more so than I was in Haiti when I was a *député*. Can you imagine me driving through the streets of New York at two o'clock in the morning... because I want to, because that's what I feel like doing? New York is half asleep and I am crossing its arteries at full speed without any passenger in the car. I pull out a cassette of Tabou Combo and I am deliriously happy. The whole city of New York is mine. New York falls asleep in my arms and the Statue of Libcrty is sad without me. The whole country is mine, baby! A guy moving full speed ahead.... the music of Tabou playing away... *How sweet it is*... wouuuuuuuu!

- Good for you, darling! But I see things differently.

- But Antoinette, darling, in the past...

- You just died in the film... You're talking about the past... You belong to history, Arnold. I am the present and in my glory, dear...

- You're wrong, Antoinette, I am in the present too.... My heart is in a sling. As Lamartine would say...

- Oh, shut up. You don't know the first thing about Lamartine.

It seems that Arnold is not succeeding in impressing Antoinette and that bothers him. He, Arnold, never court a woman who wouldn't melt like honey. This is new to him not to be in control. He is not just anybody. Arnold Gaspard, former *depute for life*, still a government official in the eyes of all the Haitians in New York, President and Chairman of the Board of all Haitian taxi drivers in New

York! Everybody looks forward to shaking his hands, calling him "Your Majesty".

How dare Antoinette …!

In a reproaching mood, Arnold starts reciting a poem:

"…You are then a new generation of women,
My dear, for Haitian women....
The ones I know, innocent and charming
Are like flowers that perfumed my garden
That breathed out love and sowed goodness
I plucked them in the wind, to make of them a
[bouquet.

The women I talk about, unique in their ways
Are the loveliest women I have dreamed of, ever.
They are loving mothers and tender spouses
Who dedicate themselves to the tasks of the
[household.

They are the incarnation of immortal love
Jealously guarding within themselves the secret
[of love.

Their wealth and glory is that of their husbands
And their only conquest, that of their beloved...

Those women are artisans of love.
Conjugal happiness is then assured

And our dear children are well protected
While, we the men, go off to struggle

Today, I am lost...!

Our women have gone out to work like us
Taking along with them their sacred charm and
[sweetness,

At the office, at the plant, malicious eyes
Steal away our secrets...

The heart is deserted; love is left to cool down.
Who will welcome us home after a long day of
Back-breaking work and endless tension?
Who will be the one to guide our children
On the way to love in this troubled world?

Who?

Listen to me, Antoinette, you who are more than
[a woman,

You, the incarnation of all charm, have all the
[gifts.

Why look elsewhere for happiness and glory,
If they are already in you, accessible, or near?

Unless you are secretly unhappy....?"

Oh, what a thunderous chord he just struck! Why did he have to say that!

- Me, unhappy? You see I have everything in life I could wish for, *darrrling.* I consider myself a queen...

- I would like to be that king...

- Arnold, if you don't want me to call my sister, the mistress of your tail, you had better be quiet this minute, or I'm going to give Nicole a call. That's enough of garbage!

So Arnold, defeated, changes the subject. He realizes he's better off leaving and go visit the young lady who used to live in Queens. Antoinette is not impressed by his sweet talk at all! What a waste of masculine energy!

From what we have learned lately, Tika and TiJan were *rich*, without their knowing it. TiJan had five thousand dollars stashed away in a turkey while Tika had ten thousand dollars hidden in a pillow case! That was a big surprise for TiJan Bonplezi. Imagine a blue collar guy who never stopped working during all the twenty years he's been in the United States and who supposedly never really possess even five cents to save his soul. Life in this "white man's country" used to mean "wash your hands and soil them on the ground." Now, all of a sudden he has fifteen thousand dollars in his hands, without counting the change!

It's as if a miracle had happened. That's the way Tika understands it to.

For people like that them who only have just a little change left over from their paycheck every month once they have pay their bills, to possess fifteen thousand dollars without borrowing it, without having to pay interest on it, without having to pay it back, is really an extraordinary occurrence.

So, for the first time in the twenty years they have been in the United States, TiJan and Tika are going to wake up one morning and go on vacation! From what could be heard on the phone while TiJan was talking with several travel agencies, they are going on a cruise called "Marilove"

Meanwhile, you remember Nicole, thc nurse in New York who married Arnold the taxi driver, Nicole is coming to Florida on vacation. Her plan is to dive in some lavish shopping with Sandra her sister-in-law and for the two to attend those elegant parties with the wives of those big shot doctors. With her tickets purchased, Nicole travels with her children in Miami! "I'm not even going to call, they're expecting me." And, why should she call ahead, TiJan and Tika never go anywhere. They are always home. With exciting anticipation, she arrives unexpected and with her spoiled rotten children at the Miami airport!

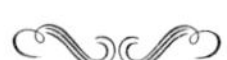

While preparations for the cruise were on their way at TiJan and Tika's, there is something else going to happen real soon at Gaston's house too. Do you remember how he had just gotten home and found the house sparkling clean, some soft music playing in the background on the stereo system, and the smell of a meal ready to be enjoyed?

Well, when Gaston arrived, Margaret was taking a shower and singing happily. Gaston approached her boudoir wondering of what could the festive occasion be. This is getting exciting, you must seat back, relax to listen. Let's catch a glimpse of what is about to happen.

Now Gaston is a little suspicious. He suspects something unusual in the house, in the smell of the food and in the openly happy mood of his companion. He doesn't know what to expect.

- Margaret, where are you? Margaret? Where are you?

- I'm coming, dear, I've almost finished getting ready.

- Getting ready to go where? Today is Saturday afternoon. What's the plan? You're going out?

- I'm not going out, Gaston. I'm not going anywhere.

Gaston enters the bedroom, he sees Margaret getting dressed. As I am observing, Margaret is putting on a beautiful dress, then, a fine perfume. She is almost done.

- Why do you have to get all dressed up and so beautifully?

Margaret doesn't answer him. She finishes dressing; she puts on some nice jewelry. With that delicate perfume announcing romance, she appears in the living room.

- Wow! Why are you looking so beautiful? Where are you going? What's up, Margaret?

- Nowhere. I'm not going anywhere.

- Then, why are you so dressed up?

- I'm not all dressed up, I'm simply dressed. Do you like my outfit?

- Of course I do. It's a beautiful dress, it looks good on you. Why are you wearing it today? You could wait and wear it one day when we go out together.

- No, I bought it to wear tonight especially. Are you free tonight?

- I'm free and available. I fine at home now. I'm not setting one foot outside again for the day.

- I'm happy about that because tonight I'm inviting you...

- Where to?

- Wait and see.

So Margaret leads Gaston to the dining room with one hand while she covers his eyes with the other. When she uncovers his eyes, Gaston sees an elegantly decorated table. On the table, in a nice *Limoges* porcelain bowl is elegantly served delicious tender pieces of conch swimming in an apricot-colored sauce topped with sliced onions. Next, au gratin macaroni slightly browned, in the center, a watercress and avocado salad contrasting with a mushroom and lima beans rice. All that accompanied with a beautiful pitcher filled with grenadine juice. Right under his eyes, a well crisped sweet potato pie sprinkled with raisins and confectionary sugar are awaiting his sudden appetite.

- What's going on today, Margaret?

Gaston doesn't get it. What day is today? Why is everything shining so bright? Is it Margaret's birthday? If it's not that, what is it? What is the occasion?

- Margaret, tell me, is it your birthday today? What are we celebrating?

- No, it's not my birthday today. My birthday was last month. Today, it's something else. It's a special occasion I created to tell you I love you.

Gaston is completely lost. What is waiting for him? Why is she making it so festive just to say I love you? He is suspicious, very suspicious.

Margaret is looking into Gaston's eyes, straight into his eyes. Gaston feels his heart beating fast as if something he never expected is happening. Margaret approaches him and kisses him and he kisses her too.

- Why are you so beautiful today? Tell me? What is going on?

- Darling, there's nothing going on. I knew you didn't have any meeting today, so I decided to cook a little dinner for us.

The fact is Gaston is somebody who is so busy, always running from one meeting to another; he never takes the time to think about his relationship with Margaret seriously. That doesn't mean he doesn't love the woman, not at all.

- My dear, look at the wonderful dishes you prepared and I had thought before coming home to eat at Tika's house…

- There's no eating at Tika's tonight. You are eating your sweetheart's food. You think I can't prepare good Haitian dishes? I can! And as for the food I cooked today, I prepared it with all my heart.

- It's a wonderful dinner! And, you cooked it yourself? No help?

- I cooked it myself....for you.

Music is playing in the background. A bolero of Haitian musician Dòdòf Legros spices the air with nostalgia. Between the aroma of soul food and the melody that bring back memory of his younger years at the family dinner table in Haiti, Gaston was empowered by his emotion. He remembers life when he was care free, problem free and full of hope and projects. A tender feeling comes upon him. He takes Margaret's hand, as if he was going to ask her to dance and she stood on her feet, ready.

The couple dances as the music becomes even more romantic. Gaston is leaning on Margaret's shoulder; they are really enjoying the bolero. The music is too good to end. Margaret rests her head on Gaston's chest. She hears his heart beating loudly. She thinks of how close they are at this moment, literally connected to each other, yet not really that close. Gaston is someone who is always far away. His soul and heart are always far away to his homeland.

The song ends too quickly but another one starts. This time it's an instrumental by Webert Sicot playing. I don't have to tell you how sweet the sounds of the saxophone sound to them. Margaret whispers into Gaston's ear:

- I love you very much, dear, I would like for us to be happy together.

Gaston awakens as if coming out of a dream; he realizes how he was just immersed into a dream about Haiti while he was in Margaret's arms. He always keeps his life as a Haitian separated from his life with Margaret, even though she is always very interested in Haitian matters.

- I love you too, what makes you think we're not happy together?

They sit down at the dining room table. Gaston seats Margaret then he walks toward a bottle of good wine that has in the refrigerator. This is a typical behavior that he would have when some of his friends come over for a politically motivated meeting.

*Mezanmi!* And they toast.

Thereupon, the phone rings. In that moment!?

The telephone rings but Gaston decides he is not going to pick up. He signals to Margaret not to pick up either. They are not going to let anyone disturb them now. Gaston is busy with Margaret and he is not going to let anyone interrupt him. That's a first!

Their conversation continues. Margaret feeds Gaston a spoonful of food as Gaston approach his glass of wine to her mouth. Mmmmmm!

Well, it seems like Gaston can be sentimental.

- Where did you get Haitian music? He asks Margaret.

- It always had them here. I bought them almost ten years ago. I have always listened to them, alone. This is the first time we listen to them together.

- What about those Haitian dishes? Where did you buy them?

- Buy them? I didn't buy any dish. I cook them all by myself, without any help.

- I can't believe it!

- Gaston, it's been a long time since I learned to cook Haitian food. A long time since I learned to dance Haitian music. A long time since I have been living like a Haitian. How is it that you realize that only today? Aren't you aware that I love a Haitian man; that I have been living with a Haitian man for close to ten years? Don't you remember that I always take part in all the marches held to defend the rights of Haitians? Every time there is something organized for Haitian rights, be it at the level of the county, the city, the House of Representatives or elsewhere, if it's to protest against the abuses toward Haitians, I'm there. Where are you on those occasions?

# CHAPTER 11

## Love without Borders

While the beautiful Antoinette was upsetting Arnold's good angel and chasing him away as if he is a distasteful mosquito, while Nicole was in Miami airport trying all the Bonplezi's telephone numbers she could find in her address book, Gaston and Margaret are living an unforgettable moment. They are deep in a conversation that makes Gaston stop and think. The fact is that Gaston has always dreamed of returning to Haiti one day, and he has always thought, Margaret is American; she is a part of his life now but not necessarily tomorrow. He intends to return to his country and Margaret will stay in hers.

Goodness, how could that woman be just a passerby in his life, if she has spent all that time with him! A man who thinks like that is making a big mistake! He needs to wake up!

The telephone rings again at Gaston's, so insistently that he decides to pick up against his heart.

- Hello.

- Hello, Gaston, this is Nicole. I have just arrived, my plane has just landed, I don't see anybody at the airport to greet me and the children. You know I didn't bring the maid and the children are going crazy...

- Nicole, you should better take a taxi because I am very busy at this moment. I cannot leave home at all now...

- Well, since you can't give me a ride, such a little favor I'm asking of you... Never mind, put Margaret on the phone, I'm sure she'll come to pick me up right away.

- I can't put Margaret on the phone. She is busy. She and I are busy now. We are talking about very serious business.

- Since when? Gaston, put Margaret on the phone right at this minute, you hear!

- Nicole, Margaret is not a drifter. She has a life. She is not available now. She is talking with *her husband.*

- Talking with *her husband? T*sssss. Really? Let me tell you, Americans will always win, ok? They never lose... Any way… Well, what am I going to do?

- What did you say?

- Nothing, nothing... Thank goodness! I am reserving a front row seat to watch this coming show… *Talking with her husband…? Ça alors!* I will have the last laugh when the vanishing act comes on!

- I have no idea what you are talking about and I don't need to either. The only thing I can do for you is pay your taxi. That's it, nothing else. Bye.

Gaston hangs up. That call disturbs him. Damn it! He was having such a wonderful conversation. Talking to himself, he says: "Look at that! Nicole has some nerve. She thinks she can use us, Margaret and me. No joke!"

Before the phone call disrupted their conversation, Margaret and Gaston's chat was getting seriously quite intense. After the call, Gaston is now somewhat upset. He cannot stand women like Nicole, who think they're entitled to everything their whim fancies upon. He thinks deep inside how different Margaret is. Margaret is a simple person. Margaret is someone special. She doesn't think she is entitled to anything from him. She doesn't think she can order him around. As he thinks about this, his heart feels great tenderness for her. He hasn't felt like this for a long time!

The food is good. Very good. There's just a hint of hot pepper in the conch. The food is excellent, neither too heavy nor too spicy. The fine wine is going to his head. He doesn't eat too much usually, but tonight...

- Would you like a dessert?

- With pleasure, Maggy.

*Maggy*?

While Margaret is cutting him a piece of sweet potato pie, Gaston gets up to grab a bottle of Barbancourt Rum Reserve to sprinkle over his piece of sweet potato pie. Margaret prefers hers with a drop of grenadine cocktail.

The music is getting even better. Now it's *Chouboulout* that's playing.

- Maggy, I want to ask you why you did all this. I mean, you prepare this special night… What is it all about?

- It means I love you. It's been a long time since I've had a chance to remind you of that. Today is a special day for me, since you came home and didn't plan to go out again right away. I am happy to share this short moment with you.

- Me too. It's been a long time since we had a good talk... I have to tell you, you are a good person... Margaret, how are things going at work?

This is the first time Gaston pauses to ask Margaret questions about her, about her daily life. It's as if they had just met.

The mystery of life!

- Everything is going well, dear. Our department is getting more funding, so we can do more research… And what about you? How was your last meeting?

- Oh, don't talk about that! Every day I hear something different. Today, I got upset because a guy made a not-too-funny joke. He said a bunch of nonsense, stating that he is no longer interested in Haiti; that he is done with Haiti…. I nearly punched his jaw. The imbecile! Imagine all that Haiti did for him! And now for him to be denying his country! Some people's eyes have no tears. He is a dead dried spoiled fish!

- Gaston, would you like for us to go and live in Haiti? Would you feel better if you were living in Haiti now?

- No, not for now! There's a lot going on in Haiti, but, in this country where we are now, an interesting part of the struggle is taking place. You know I can do more over here for now...

- Okay. Whenever you want to go, I will go with you. Whenever you want.

- How could you leave your job and your country to go and live in Haiti?

- Because that's where you want to be! Don't you know I want to be with you forever?

- Margaret? You would want to stay with me forever?

- Of course! That's why I'm here. That's why I would like for you to want to be with me too.

- I have to tell you that sometimes, when I think about you, I don't know what you would want.

- What I want? I love you; I have been living with you for a long time... I love you… I would like to spend the rest of my life with you. However, I don't know what's in your mind.

- I love you too, Margaret. I don't doubt that at all, but I'm not sure we can spend our whole life together. You are American and I am Haitian. You are White and I am Black. Those are differences that are difficult to intertwine.

- But you forget how long we have been together? How can you think like that? If you don't love the life we have together, why do you stay in the relationship?

- I love you but… I feel… a … contradiction inside me.

- Is it because you want to spend the rest of your life with a Haitian woman?

- I don't know!

- If you don't know, who does? You have to decide because I'm not interested in taking somebody else's place. I am not forcing anything on you but let me tell you this: I really love you. You taught me to appreciate and respect Haitians. You taught me to love Haiti, you taught me Creole. Since I have known you, my life is not the same any more. I really feel attached to you, to your country, to your people. I love your family. I love Tika. I have just met Edit and already I have a lot of appreciation for her. I love reading about the history of your people. I love your language. The fact that I am White and you are Black is a reality, just as the fact that you are a man and I'm a woman.

- Things are not that simple, Margaret. I sometimes ask myself if it's not a betrayal for me to consider marrying an American woman. There are so many good Haitian women. One day I will return to Haiti. And, what if I want children?

- Gaston, I am not trying to convince you, my dear. I hear you. If I'm American and you're Haitian, sure that's a difference, but that doesn't make your heart any better than mine. It doesn't make me a worse person than anybody else. If we have children, well, our children will symbolize your blue and red flag, they will show that *strength is in union*, the motto of Haiti. They will represent the union of Black and White. They will represent the inseparable union between Haiti and the United States. I will always be American because that's where I was born. You will always be Haitian because you were born there, but, the two of us together will form a new life that will become one.

- What if you mother hears you talking that way!

- If my mother hears me talking this way, she will be shocked. She wouldn't be expecting me to love and marry a foreigner, and she wouldn't be expecting me to marry you because where I am from there are not many Black people. Let me say this though: it's true my parents are not Black but they are immigrants too, they came over here on a boat too long time ago from Ireland, and their country was so poor then, you cannot imagine. My father and my mother went through a lot of misery in this rich country... Have you heard about the time of the great depression here in the United States? That was something!

- You mean your mother can understand what Haitians are going through now?

- Of course she can. She already understands it. Indeed. If you see Americans pretending that they have never been through tough times, that's might be true for now but it has not always been like it is today. Look at the history of the Jewish people. What about the Irish. These people's histories bear great analogy if not similarity with the history of Haitians. The only difference is that their trouble as new comers in that sense is over and their situation has improved considerably. Haitians are just beginning…

- You know, I like to hear you talk like that. I always knew what you're talking about now, but, acknowledging it under today's reality gives it such a powerful resonance.

- Gaston, if you love me, don't let anything blind you, don't make that mistake. I can tell you that if you love me, you will never regret it, because I love you deeply and dearly.

- Maggy, I never thought we would have this conversation, today. I know that I had always put a barrier between us. Even if we are living together, I never let down my focus on my people and I never allowed you to see that vulnerability. You're right, Maggy. In fact, there is no difference between us... Only that you're not black... But, you're Haitian in heart...I love you, dear. I really do!

- I love you too. You can't imagine how much…

The phone rings again. Margaret was just about to get up for some coffee when the phone started ringing. She is about to pick up the phone but Gaston puts his hand on it and tells her not to answer. Nobody should interrupt them again. Especially now. He has something he wants to tell her. He opens his mouth to start and sighs heavily. Is he afraid? He tries again, and, finally, opening his mouth a second time.

- Maggy, do you realize how much I love Haiti?

- I know that, and I love Haiti too.

- Do you know Haiti is the country where I want to die?

- If that's where you want to die, that's where you should die. And, that's where I want to die too.

- Do you realize that I'm a person who can sometimes neglect you because, when my country is suffering it's as if I myself is in a coma?

- Yes, I know. I have already been through most of this. I know too that Haiti deserves all that you want for it.

- I want to say.... Well, are you sure you don't want to think some more, before we go on with this conversation?

- Think more about what? No, I don't need to think about anything more. I have thought enough. I am someone who knows what she wants. I haven't been living with you because there are no other men available in my surroundings. I love you because you're the one I truly love. I have always dreamed of sharing my life with someone who had an ideal. I want to share your ideal, your dream... I hope that before we die we can see a beautiful Haiti, where all children can go to school, can go to the doctor. Where everybody has enough to eat every day. Where there's work for everybody. That's our dream. That should be our mission. I think that even if you leave me, I will continue to have this dream for your country. Haiti has suffered martyrdom. At the same time, it's a diamond in the rough but it's a diamond.

- Maggy, why are you touching the core of my heart like that?

- I don't know... And why are you rocking my soul off its moorings like that?

- I don't know! I find it strange to be looking in the blue eyes of a white woman and tell her *I love you*. I am overwhelmed, I am confused…

- There's nothing in what I'm saying that is different from what I have always felt. I have loved you for a long time, but you have always maintained a lot of distance between us. Maybe today I could say this to you: I would like you to feel that you're free to continue to live with me or not. I do not want to ask you to stay, but at the same time, if it was my decision, I would like to spend the rest of my life with you. Do you understand?

- You mean that we could...

- Huh huh, say it, go ahead. Say it!

- Like...like what...

- Gaston, if you don't feel like saying it, don't say it. I know you. However, any woman who would be in my place now would understand me. I must say that I have no proof you want our relationship to bloom and last. Our relationship thrives from day to day but has no vision for the future. I'm not asking you to love me more than you want to, but, I feel I would like, as any other woman would, to have someone who wants to share his life with me, without my forcing him to.

- You realize, Margaret, that it's something difficult for somebody like me. You know how much of a nationalist I am, and for me to appear in public with a white woman... Some people will judge me; some will say I am two faces: an Americanized Haitian nationalist…

- You should have thought about all that time we have been together. Didn't you know I was White then? Didn't you know you were Black then? Didn't you know that you're a nationalist who loves Haiti but lives in the United States? I thought we have agreed long time ago that love is deeper than that, that love is not superficial on the skin but deeply rooted in our souls?

- I understand what you're saying, and it's true we have said all this before. However, when people who are watching us see that we have crossed the line, their evil tongues will condemn me.

- Who? Your relatives? Nobody judges me because I do not allow them to. And, in my family, there's no such attitude. Didn't you see how my family welcomed you!

- People in your family are educated; they may not be racist or, they may be more subtle.

- Well, the last thing I'll say is that for me, it makes no difference whether you're Haitian, American, Chinese or Indian or else. As long as I get along with the person I love; as long as that person and I have many connections that attach us, nothing else matters. As for you, if it's a Haitian woman that's going to make you happy, good luck! Go and find one. I will be fine.

- Maggy dear, don't say that. You make me think a lot. You open my eyes to what matters. I'm looking at you at this moment, I only see a wonderful woman who I want to spend the rest of my life with. Maggy, let's get married, sweetheart. It's about time. I can no longer conceive life without you. Let's get married.

- Hmmm! I wish you could read my soul... You could see...

- Would you be glad to marry me, Maggy?

- Hmmm! Would I be glad? I would be overjoyed!

And this is how for the first time ever, Gaston came to consider marrying with Margaret. This is how he came to the realization that destiny doesn't necessarily decide things the traditional way. He loves this white woman. She is such a down to earth companion. He will marry her, that beautiful white woman.

And this is how Margaret's dream became reality.

Gaston and Margaret are getting married! Where's the vanishing act Nicole was waiting for? What an anticlimax this will be! She will fall from grace, dumbfounded!

- Darling, let's go to TiJan's, let's go now. Let's go tell them the news. I can't wait to see TiJan's reaction. Tika will be so happy! She loves you so much!

While this conversation continues to go on, Nicole is still at the airport. She telephones Sandra but there is no answer, she gets the answering machine. She leaves a message. She leaves another one. She needs to talk to Sandra right away, so they can make serious plans. Now she needs to take a taxi. Gaston told her he will pay but, should she take the risk? What if he doesn't pay her back? She doesn't want to take a taxi if Gaston is not going to pay for it. And, you never know, he might not. With all the people she has in Miami, it doesn't make sense for her to take a taxi. She needs to make a decision right away. She has been pinching the children so many times to keep them quiet that she thinks the Child Protection Services might come and arrest her for child abuse. She has tried to call over to Tika's several times without success, now she tries again and, thank goodness, this time Tika answers the telephone.

- Hello? Oh, Nicole! It's you? Where are you?

- At the airport, *machè*… Where are you? Didn't you know I was arriving any time soon?

- I knew you were to come to Florida but I can't sit by the telephone forever until you call and say "I am here." So, you are calling to say you are coming? No? You're already here at the airport? Which airport are you in? Are you still in New York?

- No, *machè*, I am at the Miami airport. I am here, my dear.

- You took a risk, Nicole, I am telling you. You didn't even let us know the date of your arrival... What if we were not home?

- Well, in that case, you would have at least called me to let me know that you wouldn't be home. The same way that you, Tika, would call me to find out if I hadn't changed my mind about coming, as you have always done... Wait a minute… You have changed, Tika…? You don't use to talk to me like that, Tika.

- I haven't changed at all, Nicole... Well, let me have you talk with TiJan, so you can explain to him where to pick you up, and we will come for you. How was your trip?

- We'll have a chance to talk later, dear. Let me talk to TiJan.

- TiJan, Nicole wants to talk to you.

- Listen, TiJan, that's not the way to do things. You're expecting company and you are not by the telephone?

- Well, the fact is you reach me now. Why didn't you ask Sandra to stay home and wait for you? She is the one you like to spend your time with, no.

- Where did you get that idea? Anyway, are you coming now?

- Where to?

- The airport! To the Miami Airport to pick me up…

- No, I can't. I have an appointment with an agency that is supposed to give me an answer. I'll pay your taxi when you get here.

- Okay, brother. Wait outside for us. I don't want the taxi to have to wait, or to think my children and I are nothings. Also, remember to give the driver a five dollar tip at least so he won't think we are nobody.

- Okay, no problem. The house is yours. We'll be waiting for you.

That's how Nicole made her triumphant arrival in Florida! As soon as she arrives to Tika's house, her children started saying, "Ma, I do not want to stay in this house!" and "Mother, why aren't we staying with Aunt Sandra?" Even the youngest one was complaining: "Mom, remember, you told us Tika's house was ugly."

Oh so it's *Tika's house*, and why isn't it Aunt *Tika's house*?

From the very minute she walks in the door, Nicole is in a bad mood. First of all, she disapprove of the way the house is fixed. People are on top of each other. Jera and Edit are also here with three children. "So, when are they going to get their own place?"

Nicole sees everything that's wrong. She tells Tika the things she needs to buy for her, where to get them. By the way, this piece of furniture does not match that one. That buffet is too old. Those curtains really need to be changed, and so on and so forth! So distasteful, this house!

- Look! You don't' have swimming pool. I came here with the children and there's no swimming pool for them. Oh, it's so boring here! Didn't you know I was coming with the children? What are the children going to do in this infernal heat?

Nicole calls Sandra from Tika's home, they will meet tonight, and they will have coffee together and plan their activity for the week.

Nicole was about to go get dressed in the expectation that Sandra will come and pick her up when TiJan tells her he needs to talk to her.

Suddenly, the doorbell rings.

Tika drops what she was doing to go open the door. You can't imagine the surprise that's waiting for her at the door. This time it's a real big surprise. A huge bouquet of flowers is being delivered at her door, right under Nicole's nose. Could it be from Paul again? You remember when Paul had surprised her with that beautiful bouquet of flowers a while ago?

But, it seems that it's not from Paul.

Tika once again is overwhelmed. The flowers might be for Nicole. She is nervous. She is even uncomfortable. She calls TiJan.

- TiJan, TiJan, come over here please, come and help me. Look at this beautiful bouquet of flowers someone has just delivered. Come here and help me, please.

- Let me see, says Nicole, what a beautiful bouquet. It must be a surprise from Arnold. Arnold sent this to me.

*Arnold?* The Arnold we know?

- Wait a minute! interrupts Tika. First, let TiJan have a look.

- What's the matter with you, Tika, can't you even read the card without calling Tijan? says Nicole mockingly to her.

- It's not that I am not able to read but when I get excited my eyes get watery and I can't see well enough to read.

- And, what is in there to make you so emotional?
- Tika, says TiJan matter-of-factly, come in with the bouquet, sit down at the table and take your time to read what's on the card. You hear?

-It's for me, she cries out overcoming with joy, *Mezanmi,* what a beautiful bouquet, TiJan was it you who sent me such a bouquet?

- Read what's written on the card, *machè.*

Tika takes the bouquet and places it on the dining room table. Nicole looks at her with irony. Only then Tika calms down enough to read what is written on the card:

"Happiness defines you,  
Tika, innocent beauty  
My eternal flower  
Every day you bloom.  
I love you for life, my hibiscus,  
You inspire endless love.  
TiJan

- *Mezanmi, mezanmi!* TiJan, what a beautiful bouquet, what a beautiful note in *French.*

- It's not in French, Tika. It's in Creole. Creole is that beautiful. Don't you feel its charm?

- *Mezanmi!* I'm going to lose my mind. What did I do to deserve all this kindness, TiJan? Thank you, *monchè. Mezanmi!* Look at this bouquet, *Mezanmi!* Come and see it, Nicole, it's for me. TiJan ordered it for me! *Machè*, this makes me so happy...

Tika cannot stand still. Oh, *Mezanmi!* What a wonderful bouquet! What a joy it is! Look at that gesture on the part of TiJan! She is so happy that she cannot withhold her tears.

This is second time in one year she receives flowers.

- What's wrong with you? says Nicole disgusted but exploding with envy. What's wrong with you what such a big deal?

- No, tries to explain Tika. There is nothing wrong with me. I'm not emotional only because of the flowers. It's because of the gesture on the part of TiJan. It's because of the immense love I feel for TiJan and the love he expresses to me. You know he is my whole life. All of my happiness is in TiJan and my three children. They mean everything to me. Oh, I feel alive! And if I die at this moment, I'll go right to heaven. I feel so happy now. I can't explain it. The reason you don't understand why I am so excited is because you receive flowers all year long. Over here, it's not something we can afford easily. Life is expensive for us and, you know, the children are growing up and it expensive to raise them...

Tika does not see that Nicole is ready to burst with envy. Flowers? Arnold sending her flowers? He sends flowers to other women.

*What does TiJan see in Tika anyway? Tss...*

- My dear, why are tears in your eyes, asks TiJan?

- I'm not crying. I'm overwhelmed with the feelings that are too much to bear. That's how I am, you know.

- Well, Tika, get ready for another shock. You are going to spend five wonderful days like a queen. I want you to have an unforgettable time and it's going to be unforgettable for me too...

... It will be our vacation, *cheri*. I don't want you to cry in our vacation either. Learn to enjoy life's pleasures. I want you to laugh, you hear, *cheri*.

- Yes, *cheri*.

Nicole listens to the two and only hear Chinese language.

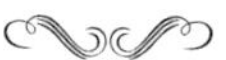

- Are you ready, Tika? Are you all set? Well, tomorrow morning the limousine is coming to pick us up.

- What, we aren't going to the port in our own car? *Mezanmi!* I already packed all our suitcases in thc trunk of the car...

- Take it easy, Tika. Don't worry. I will take of them. Now, let me take care of you. Come and lean your head on my shoulder. The limo driver or I will take care of the suitcases. When he gets here, we will worry about that.

*So you see, Tika and TiJan are ready to go on the cruise!*

The bell rings, Sandra arrives to pick up Nicole.

- Kids, Nicole tells her children, be good, okay? And, remember, go to bed early. I'll see you in the morning.

TiJan walks toward the door to open for the person who rang the bell. It is Sandra and it looks like she was not even going to step in to say hi. The two women are ready to take off. TiJan intervenes.

- Nicole, remember I told you I need to talk to you. You cannot leave!

- But, TiJan, you can at least wait until tomorrow morning, I must not keep Sandra waiting.

- Sandra will wait! And, you are going to listen to me too. First of all, you can't take off like that. Who is going to take care of your children?

- Hey, what's happening to you? Doesn't Tika usually take care of them? Tika is here, she is not going anywhere.

- That's what you say. The news is that Tika is busy. She has plan. By the way, since you have gotten here, you have upset her too much. Leave her alone! Leave her home alone, you hear! You arrived here and we are happy to see you. Don't try to change our lives because you are visiting us. There is no swimming pool here, there is no new furniture here, there's nothing here that we don't need. Yet, there are a lot of things, like love, respect and discipline to share. I hope you will appreciate those things... What I wanted to tell you is that Tika and I will be leaving...

Meanwhile, Sandra stands stunned. Sandra doesn't say a word. Nicole is under shock.

- Where are you too going to? asks Nicole.

- We are not going out tonight; we are leaving tomorrow morning early for several days.

- Not this week, I hope?

- I just say tomorrow morning early. Tika and I are going on a cruise.

- On a what?

- Yes, my dear, on a cruise. We are going to relax for a few days, five or seven days I think.

- How can you afford a cruise? Do you have money?

- Money is secondary. Tika is getting ready for the trip, so she doesn't have time to take care of the children. Edit and Jera are also very busy taking care of their own business. There's no way you can count on any of them to watch over your children.

- So, who's going to take care of my children?

- YOU. YOURSELF. There is no maid here, Nicole. You know, Tika and I, we have always taken care of ours. Now...

- What do you mean, *me*, to take care of the children, I am on vacation, no?!

- In case you don't figure this out yourself, as your older brother, I am reminding you that it is your responsibility to babysit your own children during the time you will *stay* here. Since you will be *staying* here, we assume that you will enjoy babysitting our children at the same time. Steve is old enough; you don't have to worry about him. He can take care of himself. But the girls...

- What do you mean *me* to take care of your children? I don't even know how to take care of my own!

- You can learn. We are leaving enough food for a week, for you and all the children, yours and mine alike. Ours are good children, they know how to behave and they will obey you. We are also leaving you some money for any additional expense you might have for them during the week...

- What? Jan? Me?! Babysit your children? Remember. I come here from New York for a vacation and that is how you're treating me? Sandra, do you hear that? Unbelievable!

- TiJan, interjects Sandra, this is a serious problem. Is there any way you can postpone your trip? Well... Nik, go talk with Tika, she is very understanding....

- No, objects TiJan. Waste of time. Tika has already made all her arrangements. We are going on the cruise. We are not changing any dates. And, tell me, what prevents you from babysitting our children while you're babysitting your own?

- It's not a question of not wanting to. No, the fact is, Sandra and I have made plans for tonight. Tika, can you put off your cruise? I know you'll do that for your sister-in-law.

- Nicole, don't you understand? You don't understand that Tika has her own plans. She is going on vacation, she is going on a cruise, my dear, she's counting on you, for just once, to take care of her children. It's her turn this time to count on you.

TiJan stops talking, turns around and walks toward his bedroom. Tika doesn't utter one single word. She follows him in. They go into their bedroom to relax. All of her things are already packed. She even already packed in one of her suitcases the negligee and the baby doll Margaret helped her choose. All TiJan's belongings are packed too. There is nothing missing.

It seems that everything is all set. Nicole does not know what to say or do. She is angry, she does not know on whom to vent her anger. She decides to take a last chance with Tika. Maybe Tika will have pity on her. She goes looking for Tika in her room.

- ... But, I came for a vacation! Tika, won't you do that for me?

What a confusion!

- *No*, insists TiJan. She asked you first. You are the one who is going to babysit for her. Moreover, during our absence, keep the house clean. Do not leave dishes lying around. For once, do some cooking; wash the meat and the fish carefully with lemon. Cook some beans. And do it well, you hear!

- I cannot believe it! comments Sandra. The world is turning upside down. I'm leaving, Nicole.

- No, don't go, if no one can keep the children for me here, why should I stay, I can go to your house with...

- To my house? Where?

- What do you mean, where? Your house might be the place to solve the problem.

- My dear, that is impossible. The way I see things you are not free to do the kind of activities we had talked about in our conversations. It's not going to work at all.

At that moment, the telephone rings. Gaston is calling to announce that he is coming over. Good, maybe Nicole will have another chance?

- Well, maybe hope is not lost, Nicole says. I know Margaret will accept to solve my problem. After all, didn't she take that wonderful brother of mine from me!

The house is silent, everybody is calm. Sandra is waiting with her keys in her hands. Nicole becomes pleasant again. TiJan has walked back to the living room and is quietly seated. As for Tika, she looks around innocently. It's not her fault if she is going on vacation. It's not her fault if Nicole came at a bad time. She is really sorry for Nicole.

That's how TiJan and Tika are preparing their first leisurely trip in twenty years, the first trip since they started working in the United States. They are going on a cruise. For five days, other people are going to be taking care of them, serve them food in bed; bring them whatever they want any time they want. It's the type of cruise that consulted you for your favorite dishes ahead of time and for your favorite hubbies ahead of time. Everything is designed and prepared to take you to paradise on earth. No, not on earth, on the ocean. Whatever used to be impossible before will be possible in this cruise. It's a dream that is even better than going to heaven.

For more than twenty years, their life has always mean work and work. Now, Steve's college expenses are guaranteed. Their other children have no major needs, they are still young. The parents can go and relax somewhere...

.

TiJan and Tika's life is like the life of most people they know. Having fun and spending money on luxuries is something unheard of. Their life is one of constant struggle. Now, TiJan finds it normal, since they have over fifteen thousand dollars in cash added to their savings, to take a vacation for a few of days. They have earned that right.

That's life!

# CHAPTER 12

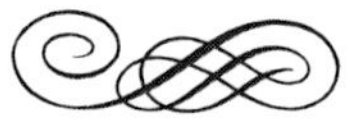

## Nothing Impossible

Margaret and Gaston have left their house and they are on their way to Tika and TiJan's house to share the news about their decision to get married. Meanwhile, Nicole is stuck with her children since Tika and TiJan's are going on a cruise. She is upset because, if Tika knew she was going on vacation, she should have informed her and maybe she could have brought her maid along. Things are even more complicated for her since Sandra, who had come to pick her up, is now standing by the door with her keys in her hand. There's only one way out. Wait for Margaret and Gaston to arrive and let them know that they will be babysitting her children. But what Nicole does not know is bigger than her brain!

At Tika's home, the bell has just rung; Gaston and Margaret appear together with overjoying smiles.

- Oh, wonderful to see you, oh, *monchè*, come in, come in... says Tika with her usual excitement toward this brother-in-law. Sister, my dear sister... she says opening wide arms to Margaret.

- Oh Gas, I'm so happy to see you, *monchè* says TiJan.

- Yes, indeed, we haven't seen each other for weeks, brother. You know, since Clinton got elected, I had so many hopes for the relationship between the United States and Haiti. But I am becoming discouraged, with all his waffling, Haiti remains at sea... That discourages me. I have almost stopped going to meetings any more. It seems as if Clinton is bluffing...

- No, *monchè*, you are a guy that analyses situations logically. Give Clinton time to work with the Congress. In my opinion, something serious will happen depending how the Congress addresses the situation. There's a lot of pressure being exerted on the government with so many Haitians in Guantanamo Bay. The American government may be worried about the false allegations that some of the incarcerated have AIDS...

Sandra is still there with her keys in her hands. She is impatient to leave. Nicole realizes she must intervene.

- How are you, Gaston? You know I just got here and without greeting me properly, you start talking politics! Come on, come here and greet me, come on, *monchè*!

- Oh, you're here! I forgot that you're here. Oh, and your children too. Oh, and *Madam* Sandra too. Oh, both of you first ladies are here together? Quite an event. Only Antoinette is missing...

- Gaston, I need you.

- If it's the money for the taxi, here...

- Thank you. You didn't have to come over for such a trifle. I have something really important to talk to you and Margaret about.

- I too have serious business to tell all of you, Gaston replies.

- Oh, today is a day for news breaking. Tika and I also have news to tell.

- Well, Sandra breaks in, I want to hear Margaret's first.

- Mine will be better said, replies Margaret, if Gaston says it.

While the crowd is deciding who will give the best news and who will give their news first, Edit and Jera are in the streets of Miami discovering the reality of the life of their people. They have kept their custom of going out for a walk together, daily. They go out together hand in hand. They feel close. Their children also walk together as if the three of them were inseparable. It's when they are all alone together that they are the happiest.

Jera and Edit have just gotten off work. The children have finished their school assignments. So, they all go for a walk, just for a walk. They go out for a whiff of air and to think, make plans, dream about a better tomorrow. They don't want to forget why they came in this country, and under what condition. Together, they are an anchor to each other. They console each other.

Ever since Edit started working at the shrimp factory, it has been like a new chapter in her life. Everybody admires her, because of her simple ways, for her knowledge, her wisdom, and the way she gives herself over wholeheartedly to help the Haitian community in her neighborhood in Florida.

Edit helps people fill applications for their residency papers. She accompanies them to look for work. She tutors children who are behind in school without charging the parents a dime. She goes and interprets for people in the Court. Look at this woman who hasn't been here six months! Even at work, everybody talks about *Sè* Edit. The manager has already named her assistant manager because she is so professional in all she does.

The Haitians at work say that their job has improved since *Sè* Edit has been there. Employees have gotten a raise. They have been eligible for health and life insurance. They have obtained the right to two days off a week instead of only one. That's what happens when there is someone educated to advocate for you. You get to know your rights and you claim them, even if you don't speak English very well. You should see how Edit treats with people.

The other day, this is what I overheard at work:

- Carmita, I haven't seen you for a long time, why haven't you been to work?

- Well, *Sè* Edit, life is kind to me. Every once in a while, my husband deserts the house and leaves me by myself with our seven children. He takes off to meet a sexy young woman. This is going on now for five years, I am really going through a lot with him, coming and going, fighting, breaking and then making up. He can never make up his mind. Now, he has come back to me in tears because he didn't know the woman had AIDS. I almost went crazy. I had to take a couple of days off to go to Fort Lauderdale to visit a *houngan*. You know I have seven children....

- *Sè* Carmita, *houngan* cannot treat or cure AIDS. This is a serious disease that bring germs into your body to destroy it and eventually kill you. This is not the time for you to throw your money away. The first thing you have to do is to get yourself tested. Stop intimacy with your husband or use protection. You do understand about condoms?

- Do you think he'll want to use them?

- *Machè,* listen to me carefully. Do you want to hear the truth? Do you want to look at life straight into the eyes?

- *Wi, Sè* Edit, I need your advice.

- First of all, you are late in the process. Since your husband couldn't decide between you and the other woman, it's you who should have made a decision. You have a right to decide to stay with him while he is seeing the other woman or not. That is your personal choice, but you can't act like a sheep not knowing what to do. If you don't want to live in a threesome, you don't have to live in a threesome. If your man love somebody else, you have the right to talk to him about it. Fighting with each other won't solve any problems!

- He used to beat me when I ask him where he had been, how come he is coming home late, whenever he arrives past midnight...

- So, he beats you too? Well, listen. First, be tested for the HIV/AIDS virus. Then, think about your situation. We can talk again afterwards.

- *Sè* Edit, help me to get that man away from me.

- If you want to get rid of him, plan to get rid of him. Anyway, go and get tested and then we will talk.

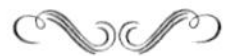

Sometimes, when some teachers send appointments for parents to show up Edit accompanies them. The other day, Martin Luther School sent for Carlo's parents. The teacher had sent several notes home but the mother didn't understand them. She put them away until the child's father would come by and read them. However, the letters were urgent. The parents were to show up at the school as soon as possible. When Edit visited and read the third letter that had come for Carlo's mother, she immediately got on the phone because the third letter was from the social services department. It was informing the parents that the child was going to be taken away of the mother's home because of child neglect. What was that? Edit accompanies the mother to the school. Let's listen what happened there:

- I am glad you came, started the teacher, talking to Edit, because this woman has been extremely uncompliant... She has never showed any interest in contacting us in spite of our repeated letters. Here is a list of complaints: Carlo wears the same shirt from Monday to Wednesday; he doesn't smell clean by Tuesday. He brings a breast of cold fried chicken and a soda for lunch every single day and this is not a way to feed a child. Carlo never brings the materials requested for his craft class to school. He doesn't go to the library on weekends for his four hours mandatory reading as all the other children do. Finally, his assignments are never completed...

- First of all, begins Edit, Ma'am, have you ever met Carlo's mother?

- No. And I do not understand her language anyway.

- Exactly, she does not understand yours either. So, there it is, to begin with, there is a communication problem. Please don't accuse her. You don't understand her and she doesn't understand you.

- *Sè* Edit, inquires Carlo's mother, what are you talking with the teacher about?

- Wait a minute *sè m*... and, turning to the teacher, Edit continues. Teacher, you have 500 Haitian children in your school, your school should have at least one person on you staff who speaks Haitian Creole. The staff at this school should also get a workshop on Haitian culture. Who is your principal?

So, Edit takes Carlo and his mother along, and they go to the principal's office. She goes and explains to the principal that if there are 500 Haitians in the school, they are not zombies, they are people. You need someone among the staff who speaks Creole to talk to those parents. American teachers need to learn a word or two of Creole; they need to learn something about Haitian culture, so they can work better with the Haitian children and their parents. She explains that Carlo's mother never knew anything about what was being written to her until now because she just translated it for her.

In fact, when Edit reads the letters to Carlo's mother, she is shock.

Take Carlo away from me!?

- *Sè* Edit, begins Carlo's mother, tell the teacher to look at me straight in the eyes and request to have Carlo taken away from me. If she does, she'll become a white zombie and be transformed into a cow that will grow black horns and be led from Jeremie to Port-au-Prince by the cattle herder for slaughter...

*Oo?*

- What is she saying? asks the principal.

- You really need an interpreter, Ma'am. Edit added kindly.

Anyway, Edit was able to help straighten out the problem, so the school did not have the child removed from the home. Edit was able to clear up the whole matter. It was after that experience that the school decided to hire a Haitian teacher. Carlo's mother learned to try to communicate better with her son's teacher. She also learned to make sure that Carlo changes clothes every day, even if the clothes are not dirty, even if the clothes don't smell bad. She also learned to send Carlo to school with a more balanced and nutritious lunch.

- What's wrong if a child wears the same shirt for three days? Carlo is a clean boy and his clothes do not smell bad. *Sè* Edit, that's racism on the part of the teacher.

- Listen, this is not racism. First of all, it is harder for a person to realize when his own clothes smell. Other people may more easily be aware of it so the best way to avoid that is to change daily. Another thing too, washing machines don't scrub clothes as efficiently as we do it manually back home. Washing machines seems to be more efficient at making the clothes smell fresh than clean. Any way, you have to try your best for Carlo to look and smell good all the time. We are not talking about heavy perfume either! That can be unpleasant as well...

- Well, *Sè* Edit, what should I do if they don't allow me to send Carlo to school with a piece of fried chicken for lunch? I don't know what else to send him with!

- Let's try to understand the problem with cold fried chicken. First of all, you most likely buy it the night before. Secondly, you put it in Carlo's lunch box early in the morning and he doesn't eat it until noontime that is more than 12 hours after you bought it. He will be eating a cold fried piece of chicken that has not been refrigerated for at least for five hours, without being warmed up. There is a great risk for that piece of chicken to spoil because at room temperature, germs must have multiplied. This can cause indigestion, stomach discomfort, diarrhea or intoxication. That big word, intoxication, can also be a killer! Anyway, fried chicken is rich in fat and can also be hard on his stomach. Are you convinced now?

Edit tries to help everyone she can in her surroundings in Miami and she enjoys doing so. She is finding a new mission and her life is slowly re-energized with so much to do, so many people to help. But now, let's go back to Tika's house to hear the interesting conversation going on between Tika, Tijan, Gaston, Margaret, Sandra and Nicole. Do you remember?

- What does Gaston have to announce? inquires Nicole. According to what I hear, from reliable source, Margaret is going to drop him.

- What are you saying? asks Margaret to Nicole. What is Nicole saying? Margaret ask around. Nicole, we have good news for you to hear. Listen. Listen to your brother...

- Listen, everyone. I have to announce to you all that Margaret and I plan to get married soon. Maybe in a week....

- Oh no, it's not true! screams Sandra in disappointment.

- What? Is that a hoax?! cries Nicole. I don't believe it... I don't... Anyway, since you're becoming officially my dear sister-in-law, I need you to babysit your little nephew and nieces. That's your official baptism into the Bonplezi family. We don't give away our family name for free. You must past the test and earn it...

- Well, interrupts Gaston, we are talking about our wedding. First, take a minute to congratulate us. It's a family event, Nicole.

-Well, declares Nicole, you, Margaret, you've been living with Gaston for such a long time that it's really not an event at all.

- Especially a marriage with Gaston, adds Sandra, in a condescending tone. Anyway, Margaret, I'll accompany you to choose your wedding dress and I will help you make arrangements to choose an elegant venue and the best catering service in town. Everything will have to be done with taste and elegance. I'll tell you everything you need to do. You know that Paul's colleagues will attend. They have to see that we, Haitians, we are not cheap when we celebrate. We must make all the snobbish people in town talk about this wedding for long time. They have to be reminded that all Haitians are not boat people...

-Ok! breaks Gaston. Maybe *you* are not boat people. Maybe *I* am not, but, *some* of us from the Bonplezi family are. Some of us from the Bonplezi Family drowned coming by boat. The blood of man Haitians just like yours and mine has spilled over the seas. The blood of some us Bonplezi has tinted the ocean. The flesh and the bones of our rclatives trying to make it ashore may have been devoured by sharks. Sandra, don't be so insensitive. Stop acting stupid. And, *tss*... I will tell you more, your blood, the blood of the Maneli family has also been washed away ashore... Ignorant! stupid, you are!

- What? shouts out Sandra with indignation toward Gaston. Blood of the Maneli family? No way! You must be crazy! There is no member of the Maneli family that has even intended to come to the United States as boat people. A Maneli coming to this country illegally? No way! Not even in your worst nightmare, you hear! You know very well that our family...

- Sandra, I have to teach you a little Haitian history. I owe you that! Not today, but, one day, I will. Anyway...

- Gaston, protests Nicole, you should not say aloud that some of our family members are boat people. Why do people have to know about that? Dirty laundry should be washed at home, as we say in Haiti...

- And what do you do with dirty tongues? replies Gaston... really upset. Listen, listen to me carefully. Every Haitian...I have said this before, damn it..., I will say it again...

- Saint Jude and Saint Charles Boromee, bring peace right now under this roof, exclaims Tika, overwhelmed with too much emotion. *Mezanmi!* Calm down every one. Everybody, come to the table. Let's get something to eat. Come and have some papaya milk shake if you don't want to eat.

- See....Tika is really frightened, TiJan observes. Don't you see, she has to call upon another saint to come assist Saint Jude in this heated conversation? Turning with a sense of humor toward Tika, *Madanm*, it seems as if you're losing faith in Saint Jude since that business about...

- TiJan, stop that you hear! I don't like this! You know, let's change conversation. Well, I have a bottle of wine in the fridge. Let's open it. What do think, TiJan, let's celebrate Gaston and Margaret's good news. I have been praying for this event for so long!

- Well, add TiJan, our news is that Tika and I are going on a cruise. We're going on the *Marilove* for five days. Of course, we're coming back on time for the wedding, Gaston. In a week! as for you, Nicole, as I have already told you, we left you food in the refrigerator and spending money for the children. Wherever you take your children, you can take ours too. You have the key to the house; we know you'll be delighted to spend some time around here...

- Well Nicole, Sandra says, unconcerned, in that case, dear, we can't make plans together anymore. What can you do if you have to take care of the children? Nothing! Forget about the grand opening ball tomorrow night!

- My news is TiJan's news. We are leaving tomorrow morning early for the cruise, in the name of Saint Jude, offers Tika. We forgot to ask you, Nicole, what news you have for us?

- I have no news at all. My plans are now spoiled, unless Margaret...

- Listen, interjects Gaston, cold and firm. Do not ask Margaret any favor she wouldn't ask you, do you hear?

- Sandra, inquires Nicole, cornered and desperate, what if I go to your house? Sincerely, I don't want to stay in *this house*. I don't' want to stay here. I *want* TiJan and Tika to find someone to take care of *their* children.

- Well... say Sandra, hesitantly.

- You know, I am going back to New York!

- Well, Nicole, if you are going back to New York, I am leaving, decides Sandra... No reason to waste time here. Looking at Margaret, she continues. As I was telling to you, Margaret, show them! Make your wedding the talk show of Miami. Show everybody, every single human being in Miami, who you are. Make them all talk about this wedding till they're all sick of hearing about it. Personally, I want a video to send to Haiti. My family has to see how Paul's family is progressing in the United States... You know, we must keep the reputation... We have to be elite wherever we go.

You remember that TiJan's house is the epicenter of the whole family. No surprise that, in the middle of this awkward moment that another family member will arrive. Paul, you remember, Paul, Sandra's husband, just finishes his long work day at the hospital. As a reflex when he is tired and nostalgic of a quiet life, he is heading to TiJan's house for a fresh brewed cup of coffee. Tika always has a hot pot of coffee on the stove. Paul walks in with the anticipation of fresh coffee when he overhears his wife talking boastfully about the *Haitian elite*.

- Good evening, ladies and gentlemen. Oh, look! Nicole! What are you doing here in Miami? What a miracle!

- Well, I came for fun but now, I'm going back in the next available airplane since there is nobody who can babysit for me.

- Really? What, Sandra, can't you arrange that for Nicole? Can't you ask our children's nanny to...?

- No Paul. Out of question, objects Sandra. Why do you have to meddle in this matter, Paul?

- What? You have somebody? A possible babysitter? asks Nicole, desperate to find someone.

- Oh, Nicole, don't listen to Paul, you hear. I am telling you, you didn't bring money for that. Who would pay this expensive woman?

- The people who are to blame have money to go on a cruise, declares Nicole. Sandra, you know very well I can afford to pay a helper. Call that person right away. I will hire her. I am not cheap when it comes to spending money for my children...

*Really? Since when?*

- How come, comments TiJan, you're too cheap to pay for your own taxi ride? In fact, there's a name for that.

- Oh, TiJan, agrees Gaston, don't try to find a word for this behavior. I will tell you, there's a kind of people who disregard everyone around them. Nobody count but themselves. They alone count. These people tend to get along among themselves as long as everything goes well. If one ever has to spend a dime on the other, their relationship evaporates and they pull away. It's worse than *dog eat dog*; it's the *criminal stealing from the thief.*

- Let's drop the conversation, suggests TiJan. Let's forget about our differences. Everybody let's be happy. Let's make life beautiful again. Nicole is staying over. Gaston and Margaret are getting married. And, my wife and I are going on a second honeymoon.

- How can you still go to the cruise, objects Nicole, I just I told you I am not staying here to babysit your children!

- We'll find a way, replies Tika ingenuously, and if we have to stay, we will.

- Oh no, Tika, Margaret insists, you are not staying. You can go. I will take care of the children. They are good children and I love to be with them.

- Of course, seconds Gaston, my wife and I will take care of the kids. Everything will be ok. Go have some rest.

- Huh, responds Tika, Gaston, I am listening, you're already calling Margaret *your wife*? You guys, you are in a hurry! Wait at least till the wedding bands are blessed.

Nicole gathers all her belongings and leaves with her children to Sandra's house. Paul puts some of Nicole's baggage in Sandra's car and some in his car. He rides alone in his own car and the two women ride together in Sandra's. Now that she knows Nicole will be paying, Sandra doesn't mind letting Nicole come to her house. They're good friends again and start gossiping about Tika. Again and Again!

- So, says Nicole, the little lady is going on the Marilove?

- Yes, *ma chère*, Sandra replies, do you see how life is, who could have imagined it? My mother would have died of indignation to know that her daughter isn't the first one to go on this cruise!

- Oh. Let's her go and chew on her bones. Oh, Sandra, I have an idea. What if we go in this Marilove cruise on the Marilove too? I have all my credit cards with me. I'll pay for you. Let try to find a last minute deal...

- You're paying for me? Good! Let's go spoil their honeymoon. That is too much for Tika!

- I agree. That's too much! bursts out Nicole.

When they arrive to Sandra's, after Paul finishes unloading all the suitcases, the first thing Sandra tells him is:

- You know Paul, Nicole and I we are leaving the children with you. We have decided to go on a cruise.

- No, Sandra, you are not going. You are not going to this cruise! Leave Tika and TiJan in peace. You are not going to bother them. You are a curse, my dear! Go learn something that isn't destructive... you spoiled brat!

- Oh Paul? Who are you talking to like that? You'll see. I will go anyway.

- Sandra, you are staying and that's an order!

And that is how the conversation ended. We will find out in the morning how the story will end. Would Sandra and Nicole take off to the *Marilove* at the last minute? Tomorrow can be worse because Antoinette is coming to West Palm Beach. She, of course, gets along with Sandra and Nicole. There will be quite bit of gossip circulating. Antoinette had called Tika minutes ago and said on the phone:

- ...I'll leave Palm Beach tomorrow morning, right after the filming. Don't panic, girls, I'm coming. And I am coming ready to put back everything in their place. I'm coming. I'm going to set things straight. I have already spoken with TiJan; he knows not to leave before I arrive. Good night, darling. Say hello to Nicole. All will go well.

What kind of a turn of events is that? What does Antoinette mean? TiJan will wait for her *before* leaving! Why? Watch out that those ladies don't spoil everything!

# CHAPTER 13

## Marilove

Tika and TiJan left on their cruise. Nicole, after the initial shock to find out that Tika had her own plans, thanks to Paul and Sandra, is finally able to find a place to stay with her children. She is at Sandra's house.

Margaret and Gaston are running around making all the arrangements for their wedding, which they want simple and private, at Tika's house, the day after Tika and TiJan will return from their cruise. Edit and Jera continue to take care of their own business but once in a while they give a hand too.

Tika and TiJan are spending wonderful days together, even better than they could have imagined. Their vacation is so unforgettable that I have to make the time to tell you about it. Imagine an extravagant night, the last cruise party, the last night. The *Marilove* is a big cruise company that offers unimaginable marvelous vacations. Can you believe there were two thousand five hundred people on board? Tika, as usual, is shy and intimidated, but, for this last night, TiJan convinces her to attend the ball.

- Tonight is our last night on board, we have to go dancing, Tika.

- Oh, TiJan, I don't feel comfortable to dance in front of all those people. So, so many people! I haven't even seen other Black couple on board yet.

- I don't care if there are or there are no other black couple on board. We paid to join, just like anybody else. Tonight is the closing ball. Do you hear, *cheri,* remember, this is the first time we go on vacation? Let's enjoy it, forget about everybody else. You are, Tika, the queen of my heart; the most beautiful woman in the world; the girl I made a woman. *Madame, me ferez-vous l'honneur?*

- *Mezanmi,* TiJan! Now you're talking to me in French! You are trying to convince me… but, I feel embarrassed. What clothes should I wear? I have already worn everything I brought.

- Not to worry! *Madame*, close your eyes and be surprised! Tada! Here!

- Oh, TiJan, where did you get that beautiful dress?

- I just bought it at the boutique on board and, see… I got you flowers too.

- Oh, Jan! Oh, Jan! tell me it's not true, tell me it's not me, it's not me here on this ship about to put on this beautiful dress. Tell me it's not me here listening to you saying those loving words… Tell me it's not true, it's not for Tika all that...

- Yes, it is for Tika. Tika, this is not a lie. This is not a dream. This is reality. It is reality without limit between you and me, between that little girl who they called Tika and that woman who came to the country of the white man with all of her courage and who has become the beautiful princess before me today. This is the reality of this beautiful Creole woman before me, offering me the purple and luscious fruit of her lips.

- *Mezanmi*, where are my children?! Where are they! I feel too much happiness around me. I need them here with us to share the moment. Where is Steve and the other children? Where are you, my son, to see your mother floating happily as a kite in the sky?

- You are happy, my wife, and that makes me happy.

- So, TiJan, when you speak of love, you speak French?

- I didn't realize I was speaking French, Tika. The vodka must have gone to my head. I just feel how happy we are together. It's no longer common nowadays to see people who have been married for over fifteen years still be in love. I realize how much I love you; I have always been in love with you, even if I haven't had a chance to say it to you or to take you on a cruise like this one. I love you, Tika. You're a rare treasure!

- Me too, TiJan, I look at you and feel I am more in love with you than ever, I love the gray hair growing on your head; I love the lines that are forming under your eyes, they tell our story… Our life story

*Has Tika taken some vodka too?*

- You don't think I am getting old?

- Old? If it is the way you are getting old, keep on going old! I love you, honey.

The couple went to the ball. Tika went dressed in the gown TiJan had bought for her. Attractive she is. And she is no longer shy or embarrassed. She feels that she is a beautiful woman. Her husband loves here. She feels that she has fulfilled her fondest dreams. Soon, her son is going to Harvard. She is on a cruise. She has nothing to apologize for.

The music is playing softly, you know, a nice American music. Each woman resting lightly on the shoulder of her partner. The boat is coasting along with the music circulating as would a subtle fragrance permeating the ballroom, a scent of love and joy. Tika rests her head on TiJan's shoulder.

Eventually, the music style changes. The orchestra plays a calypso. Tika looks around and sees the dancing mood becoming more enlivened. Then, the orchestra plays a tune from Martinique. Oh, Martinique! So close to Haiti! Tika feels the music going into her veins. She lets go of TiJan's hand and allows her body to move with the music. TiJan too is showing off his dancing skills, burning the floor under him. And, now they are playing a Haitian tune. Tika is swept off her feet.

That's how a couple dances when happiness set the tune. That's also how a woman can be beautiful when she feels loved by her man. That too is how a man can feel fulfilled when his woman loves him. What a wonderful thing love is!

Where would Sandra, Nicole and company have fit in this picture?

- *Mezanmi*, TiJan, the music is so good!

- *Mezanmi*, how long hasn't been since I danced like this!

- Oh, the music is stopping? ...Oh no, it's starting up again.

- That's the way it is, that's life.

They had been dancing with so much excitement that they did not realize how many people were looking at them. The crowd had formed a circle around them admiringly. Other couples in love stopped to admire this happy black couple dancing. People stopped dancing to gaze at Tika and TiJan. Wow! That couple knows how to dance. Wow! Magnificent! Wonderful! What a beautiful couple they are!

Finally the music came to an end. At least a thousand people were applauding them with admiration, envy and friendliness. Several people came over to congratulate them and shake their hands. They were all strangers, men and women they did not even know, they never met. People in the cruise where in a loving and happy mood.

- What a nice couple you are. Where are you from?

- You dance marvelously, where are you from?

- We're Haitians, answers TiJan proudly.

- Really? I didn't know Haitians like to dance...

- Yes, we're from Haiti, Tika raised her head up to answer.

- Do you miss Haiti? I am told that life is awfully rough down there for many people...

- Indeed, replies TiJan, but it is also a wonderful place to live. A place with kind, strong and loving people, in spite of the problems.

- Tell us a little about voodoo and the tonton macoutes, asks a man in his late sixties...

- Not tonight, Tika replies, some other time, we could talk in length… Here is our telephone number. We'll be delighted to tell you about Haiti. Our country is a poor but it's a wonderful place. The people are warm and kind. Our culture is rich, you know. Our music is passionate. Our paintings so vivid. But, let's talk about that some other time... Enjoy the night!

- Congratulations, you both dance to perfection!

- Thank you, replies TiJan, thank you.

While Tika and TiJan are talking with the crowd, a voice announces that a special prize is to be presented right now to the couple who had electrified the floor. Tika and TiJan are the winners! They walk across the dance floor to receive their prize. A ten-day trip to Europe. Europe!?

*Europe? You hear that?*

During his thank you speech, TiJan mentioned that their eldest son, Steve, is going to Harvard University. His son is dreaming in becoming a physician. He got warm applause and congratulations.

While the cruise is winding to an end, in Miami, Margaret and Gaston are just done calling few rare friends to invite them to their wedding. No a big wedding. Just a family get together. Sandra and Nicole are already making fun of them. Compared to their wedding, there is nothing to talk about this one!

- What a strange taste! says Sandra with disgust, getting married privately, as if you had something to hide. Don't you think?

- You know Gaston is cheap; he doesn't want to spend money on the woman!

- *Ma chère*, do you remember when I got married? That was a wedding! The whole main square of Petionville was packed, people dressed in finery, in the latest style. And wasn't that original of us to get out of the limousine and walk across the square so the crowd could admire me and guess the length of my train? That was something… But this marriage...!

- Yes, Sandra. It was a beautiful wedding, with so much class. But, you know, mother wasn't really very happy that day. You know how older people are. The high heels were too much for her to stand on.

- Well, she couldn't have avoided that! My dear, society is society. It was out of question for Marie Lucie to wear quarter height heels for an event like that. It's the price you have to pay when you marry into high society. I wouldn't have let everyone in Petionville criticize me for marrying cheap.

- Be careful, *ma chère*, be careful. The Bonplezi are not anybody. We have class, too. Besides, Paul was already a doctor when you married him!

- You don't understand, Nicole. You see, I know that Paul is a doctor, but, my parents, you see, they still resented my choice. It was a lot for them to swallow when I told them about Paul. For them to accept him, I had to add a lot of frosting on the cake....

- Well. I think that Paul did the same as you did. He poured lot of frosting on his cake when he told my parents about you. I can't forget how he had to plead with Papa to persuade him to accompany him to ask your father for your hand. Papa always felt that Paul should have married an educated woman, someone with a profession, you see.

- He's just an upstart, your father! Well, and what was your mother's profession?

- My mother graduated in Home Economics. She founded the most popular domestic arts school in the country... My mother was always a woman who had ten useful and productive fingers. She wasn't the type of woman to sit around in a fabric store all day.

*Well, the two ladies are going at it, with tongue and teeth!*

While they are eating each other trying to prove which of the two is greater, which of the two is the elite and which one is the upstart, the phone rings. Nobody answers, so Paul picks up. It's Antoinette, his snobbish sister.

- Hi, darrling, how are you?

- Oh, when I hear the word *darrling* I know it's that actress.

- Oh yes, I am in Sarrrasota for a culturral perrformance. What's new? What interesting news is happening in your family?

- Well, Gaston and Margaret are getting married tomorrow. Tika and TiJan are arriving tonight from a cruisc. Yves and Ana Maria are coming to Gaston's wedding. It's going to be a real family reunion. Are you coming?

- Well, that depends. You know....I have another plan… I am invited...Will Gerard and Edit be there?

- Of course, Edit will be the bridesmaid. I have to tell you that Edit is working now and so is Jera. We have a big surprise for them. We have been able to get them their legal permanent status in this country.

- Darrling, I am not coming. Don't remind me of those boat people who come into this countrry illegally. Coming to this countrry without a visa? Imagine! It's a national scandal.

- That is the reality of many Haitians here. Can't you use your brain to understand why?

- Not for that. No! Let me talk to Sandrra.

Paul calls Sandra. Antoinette's conversation always upsets him. What kind of a sister did God give him! She is just like Sandra and Nicole. Three snobs! And they don't even imagine how upsetting they can be.

- Sandra? Telephone!

- Who is it?

- Your friend, Antoinette.

- Oh, hello, Anni, where are you?

- Darling, I am very clossssse by, right here in Sarasssssota for a prrremierre, you see. Tell me therre is something interrresting going on and I'll fly right into Miami!

- My dear, nothing is happening. It's perfectly dead here. Only boring things going on.

- What about *that* wedding? And what about that bridesmaid choice! Can you believe it? What a perrfect lack of taste! Gaston should have given Edit time to become a little morre polished. Boat people being brridesmaid! Distasteful!

- Well, to tell you the truth, she is not as bad as she sounds. Since she was a teacher in Haiti, she seems to be quite refined. No matter how much you may hate to admit it, sometimes you just can't deny the facts. But, listen, the wedding will be completely private, just for the family, and even, just for the close family! That tells you…

- Then, it's not worth it. Why make the trrip for so little. Gaston should have told me. If it's a question of money, I would have paid the expenses.

- Listen, at least, if the reception was being held in an elegant venue, somewhere elegant in Miami, at least, we could have shown what kind of Haitians we are! We would have made people's eyes bleed with envy. They are missing an extraordinary opportunity... But, listen, get ready to laugh. The wedding party is at Tika's!

- Huh? That ends it, perriod! In any event, I am not coming. Therre is no audience for me to call this an event. You know I like to feel the vibe of the public. The Bonplezi family is not a motivating audience for me!

- You see that too. That's what I was telling Nicole but she is not totally convinced.

- What, Nicole is with you?

- Huh, she is with us for the moment.

- Let me talk to her.

Sandra calls Nicole for Antoinette. In the conversation, the ladies decide that there is nothing interesting happening in Miami; that Gaston's wedding is going to be a low class celebration; that the thought of Tika going on a cruise is so grotesque that it shouldn't even be mentioned. There's more happening in Sarasota where a handsome hunk from Gerard Depardieu's entourage has asked Antoinette if she is free tonight. Sandra and Nicole find the gallantry tempting, they both decide to go and visit Antoinette in Sarasota.

They decide to let Paul go to the wedding with the children. Paul is delighted because he is concerned that those women can spoil the moment. He drives them to the airport so they can go on their Depardieu adventure! Good bye!

Tika and TiJan's return is uneventful. Upon arriving home, Tika notices that Edit had cleaned the house. Everything is ready for the wedding.

On the next day, the day of the wedding, Paul arrives very early. He is the best man. Margaret's family has arrived. They are staying in a hotel at the corner. All Tika's, Edit's, Nicole's and Sandra's children are having fun together. The children are not even aware that their parents are dealing with some deep dysfunctions.

The phone rings. Solanges is at the airport. She says she is taking a tax. Nobody needs to bother coming to pick her up. She will arrive with Yves and Ana Maria who are landing soon from California. Everybody who wants to attend will be there.

Carl Henri, Antoinette's husband, can't make it. He is busy conducting serious business in Chicago. Arnold, Nicole's husband, is traveling; he is on a trip to Haiti because someone has offered him a new *deputé's* job, without him being elected. He says if all goes well, he'll be back on time for the wedding.

One person, who would like to be present but will not, because he is busy in France. That's Dieudonné, one of Gwo Sonson children's outside the marriage. Therefore, a brother among the Bonplezi, even if he is from another mother. He always likes to attend family events, but, he did not have sufficient time to make arrangements. He has, however, promised to call on the day of the wedding along with Lise, his wife, to congratulate the bride and groom. Dieudonné was a child born outside the family but he has never forgotten how *Manplezi*, his father's wife and mother of his siblings, has allowed Papa to acknowledge him as his legitimate son. This subject is another story we will save for another occasion...in another book.

Everything is ready. Jera is there not saying a word. It is such a joy for him to see all the people he loves together. It reminds him of the time he planned long a large about taking the risk of coming to this country in an illegal boat. He remembers imagining his family. He remembers imagining his arrival here. He never imagined the reality of his family here, fractioned in social classes. He never imagined the family separated into two camps, bourgeois and non-bourgeois. Today, the bourgeois camp is not present! Wow!

Solanges arrives, she is so happy. At the airport, he meets Yves, the younger of the Bonplezi.

- *Mezanmi, Mezanmi*! What a joy to see all of you! Aren't Tika and Tijan lucky to have such wonderful weather yearlong!

- My dear, objects Yves, always fresh, Canada is not cold at all. You're old that's all.

And of course, there is that Ana Maria, Yves's eternal girlfriend.

- *Mira, amorcito, Adónde sera la boda?* asks Ana Maria.

- *Aquí en la casa de Tijan. Aquí mismo*, explains Yves.

- *Aquí? Ay, por Dios. Entonces, no es una boda...es un casamiento chiquitito.*

Tika, as usual, in heavens when the family is around.

- *Mezanmi*, Tika, exclaims Solanges, it's been so long since we have been together. Where is my godson? Where's Jera? Oh, *monchè*, my brother! Oh, Edit! And the children! I'm so happy to see you.

A very special day...

-Yves, start making the video for me, ask Solanges. These are such precious moments that I want to cherish forever...

- Steve is in town, answers Tika to Solanges, he is on his way home. I sent him on an errand. Wait till you see him. He has grown so much! He is tall and handsome. You know, he is leaving the nest! He is going away to college next week. He is going to Harvard...

- Exciting! Solanges, asks Edit, tell me about you?

- Oh, *mezanmi*, Edit! I feel like I am dreaming. Look at you Edit, look at you! You are more beautiful than ever. Let me hug you, dearest... Look at you! You're like a precious jewel. Such a strong woman! Such a rock! They tell me all about what you have been doing for undocumented Haitians here. *Machè*, I want to congratulate you. You are a role model! Gerard too is doing great things, huh?

- Jera is doing okay. We are hanging in there. We feel that we have a mission to accomplish here in Miami, and we will fulfill it.

- Paul, inquires Solanges, where is Sandra?

- Oh, she is out of town. She had to go somewhere with Nicole.

- Oh, I see...

While I am paying close attention to Solanges and her connection with the family members around her, all the guests arrived for the wedding. Solanges keeps looking at Jera, she is so happy to see him. Steve has returned from the errand. TiJan is calm and reflective. Everything is ready, everyone is ready. They all gather in the living room waiting for the justice of peace to come and officiate. Even Arnold is back from Haiti. He did not get the promised job. The person who had offered it to him is now in hiding, so Arnold is happy to return to New York driving his taxi cab after the wedding. Besides, he doesn't need a *député*'s job, he says. Perhaps if it was a prime minister's position!

*Really? Really!*

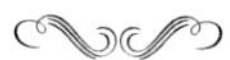

The marriage was celebrated. Very simply. Margaret's family blended imperceptibly. They participated with friendliness and even timidity. At some point, Margaret's father got up for a toast:

- To the joy of Margaret and Gaston. May God bless you! May God bless all of us!

Margaret's mother and two of her brothers took part in everything. When necessary they ask for translation.

Otherwise, they are well involved, enjoying the moment The younger brother suggests that both families gather again at his house in Ohio for this coming Christmas.

*I won't miss that! You better believe it.*

The family has a great time together. The reception is a buffet catered from a nice restaurant nearby. Everyone chooses the dishes they like. Margaret parents tries most of the dishes. The food is delicious and I want to leak my fingers but I refrain from such foolish idea.

Margaret's father helps Tika in the kitchen. Her mother is in the living room talking to Paul about Haitian paintings. The lady is well informed and well read. She is eager for Margaret and Gaston to have children

- I can't wait to cherish these assorted chocolates. I usually like to see mixed race kids. They are the future of the universal world. My grandchildren will be my favorite ones.

- You are a lovely mother-in-law, compliments Paul. How shall I call you?

- Please call me Dee. My seven grandchildren and their friends call me Nana and I love it.

We are at the end of the reception. Simply and lovely. One by one, everyone greet and say goodbye. Solanges goes to the airport hotel for the night. Yves and Ana Maria are heading to Hialeah to spend the rest of the weekend with Ana Maria's family. Gaston and Margaret volunteer to accompany her family to their hotel.

Now everyone is gone. Edit, Jera and TiJan and Tika cleaned up and got the house back to the way it was before. Tika is about to join the threesome in the living room. She has so much to tell Jera and Edit about her cruise. She wants them to plan one just like that one day. was about to sit down to recount her beautiful adventure on the cruise.

Tika castes a last glance at the kitchen and notices a message on the counter. Someone has called earlier from Haiti and she is urged to call back immediately.

She calls. She learns that her mother Tisiyad died the night before. The news brings a sharp pain to her, just to imagine that while she was dancing her soul out; her mom was dying in Haiti. Her mood switches immediately to sadness and the tone of the house gets somber.

From joy to pain. Life is that way!

# CHAPTER 14

## The Death of Tisiyad

Tika flies to Haiti two days later. It has been fifteen years since she has been there. She feels like a foreigner. GwoSonson and Manplezi are at the airport to pick her up. She gets in the rented jeep that is driving her to Dèyè Lagon, the tiny community in the south side of Haiti where she is from. Tika wasn't prepared for her mother's death. Still in shock, she doesn't even cry. In the rush to attend the funeral because there are no funeral home in this town and corpse must be buried within thee days maximum, she barely had the opportunity to give instructions to TiJan. No food shopping, not even time to help Steve preparing for his flight to Boston. She left home lucky to have found a last minute ticket to Port-au-Prince. Now, on the main long road toward her hometown, she has plenty of time to think of her husband and children, left without her loving and caring attention. And Steve, the cherished and only son is leaving for Harvard this week!

It's only upon her arrival at Dèyè Lagon that Tika is conscious that she is really here for her mother's burial. As soon as she arrives, she hears the first wailer's lament:

- *Mezanmi*! Oh, look at Tisya! look at Tisya! It's my mother's death that bring you here. Here she is, mother! Here come your successful daughter! Here she is, mother, to honor your spirit. Cover her with your soul, mother! Look, look upon us, look at Tisya yes, mother, ohhhhhhh! She comes to say good-bye to you!

- Oh Anayiz, cried Tika, Anayiz my sister! What situation we are in, now! Ana! Beniswa! *Mezanmi*, Beniswa! Beniswa! Hold me, Beniswa!

It is as if Tika had never left her hometown, that tiny community in the countryside that has only one road. It doesn't take an hour for Tika to feel at home, although she left her hometown since she was thirteen to attend middle school in Port-au-Prince. All that time she has been in the capital and then left for the United States collapse in her memories as she reconnect with her people and face the depart of her mother. Tika is transformed back into Tisya, her childhood nickname.

- Yes, cried Beniswa, melted with emotion, that's the way it is. Your old woman was fine until Thursday. Friday, she woke up, fell of her bed, and suddenly she is gone. We were waiting for you to call your husband family so they could in turn inform us when you were coming. There is no burial of Tisiyad without you! You know that. You know there isn't any morgue here but, we kept her day and night with ice bags. There couldn't be burial without you, Tisya! No! There couldn't be any burial....

All of Tika's extended family is gathered in this *lakou*, this mini village where everyone lives close to each other, in the same compound. As soon as Tisya has arrived, everyone put on their black or somber clothing. Covered in black from head to toe, everybody circle the open casket. The funeral, I guess is starting.

Tika stands at the foot of the casket to have a good look at her deceased mother. And the wailing begins again.

- Help me, Tika proffers as if chanting, help me! My dear mother is gone. She is gone for real. What do I see here. I am facing the truth. *Mezanmi*, help me, everyone! Moootthhheeerrr! Mooothernrr! You didn't give me a chance to do anything for you. Moooother!

- Woy! Anayiz interjects. Woy! Hold me! Hold me, woy, woy, woy! Recently, mother has been asking about you Tika all the time. Tika, Tisya, woy, woy, hold me, *Mezanmi*!

- *Marenn*, the second wailer continues, you are ahead and we are behind you. What situation do you leave us in, *marenn*! Who is going to take care of us now, *marenn*?

- Woy, begins the third wailer, let's tie our belt tight to take the blow! It's so hard! It's hard...You, *matant*! You're gone, you're gone, you're gone! Gone for real? No way! *Mezanmi*, I cannot bear this!, woy, woy, woy, woy!

- Lamèsi, Lamèsi, calls out another wailer, come relieve me. The goat is ready... I have to go fried the pork... I don't want the fire to die out before the rice is ready....

Lamèsi comes over, and takes over the wailing. Further down in the backyard, some people are enjoying themselves. Some are playing cards, others dominos.

- *Mezanmi*, cries the new wailer, let's stop crying. My God, the old lady was always cheerful, she always said "Don't cry when I die." Let's sing instead:

*Dede, Detitit,*
*De Manman, Ki Manman?*
*Manman Poy, Ki Poy?*
*Poy Nan Bwa. Ki Bwa?*
*Bwa Gayak, Ki Gayak?*
*Gayak Jon. Ki Boyo?*
*Boyo Nan Bwa. Ki Bwa?*
*Bwa Gayak O*

*Ki Gayak?*
*Gayak Jon O O O O*

*Pwonpwonp Chi*
*Pwonpwonp Chi*

*Ala traka Pou Anatol*
*Yon Gep Panyol*
*Bobo L Nan Dyol*
*Etan L Ap Keyi Kowosol O*

*Pwonpwonp Chi*
*Pwonpwonp Chi*

The money Tika has bought for the funeral is all spent. Every single penny is gone. After the burial, her sister and her cousins went shopping in the next town open market. They came back loaded with bags full of food. Meanwhile, her uncles and a couple of neighbors have slaughtered pigs, goat, chicken and most living animal in their farm to cook a super heavy meal to celebrate the life of the deceased and the ability of her offspring to throw a huge party on her memory.

After being so supportive crying with us for three days and carrying the coffin to the end of the property for burial, close neighbors get themselves comfortable in the backyard, ready for the well-deserved feast. For now, they are served plenty of *clairin, tranpe, babankou* and other local alcoholic mixtures. Soon, more people of Dèyè Lagon who believe they deserve a rich tasty meal in memory of the deceased will show up. Tisya's family has only a couple of hours to finish cooking and show their *good manners* to the village. Besides, Tisiyad is not a regular peasant; her daughter is a *well-established* Haitian-American in Florida!

Soon, as traditional, a long line of neighbors and even uninvited people from far away will be walking in the compound, paying respect to the family. They will also come to serve themselves tasty meals that one gets only after big shots funeral.

Now, the aroma of tasty juicy goat is mingling with *griyo*, well-seasoned fried pork that goes well with steamed rice and beans. Men drinking heavily may prefer *bouyon*, a type of rich tasty stew that is perfect for an all-night never ending domino and *bezig* games. Women dressed now in white gather in small groups telling stories, exchanging gossip and looking furtively from time to time in Tisya's direction, trying to evaluate how much of Dèyè Lagon she has left in her demeanor.

The ambiance now is more of a life celebration. Laughter, Christian hymns, pagan songs tainted with spicy jokes and even possible loa's attack are in the air. A long line of people is now standing in rows of two waiting to fill up their plate with a good yummy food. Lot of food on the table since the night will be long.

At the least expected time, a confident voice raised his glass and with a drunken voice claimed with much confidence: "What a wonderful funeral! Tisiyad went to a peaceful life and leave us with the torment of being drunk! Amen!"

Death is a celebration. The countryside of Haiti is known to celebrate death generously.

There is little left of the griyo and of the goat. A new group of cooks is now frantically preparing some creole chicken. I was so busy walking around and getting acquainted with this side of Tika's family that I missed the feast. There was a plate of food well covered on the table but I was advised by Anayiz that this is the food left aside for the spirits.

*Bon! Men bagay la!*

It is now five o'clock the following morning. I have eaten plenty of chicken, fried plantain and akra. Everybody has eaten more than they need to, everyone is full. Most people are gone. The family has fed the village and they will be remembered for that feast for long time. Whoever did not come for the ceremony celebrated by the pagan priest may have sent an empty bowl to be garnished and sent back to them.

The house is becoming calm. Everyone is tired and hoping to sleep for one or two hours. They must be awake when Tisya will leave to return to Port-au-Prince.

The roosters have decided it is time to wake up. Before the sun, Anayiz and her cousins are awake making the fire, preparing coffee and making some casava bread for Tisya. The house is sparking clean. Beds have white sheets. The table has a white tablecloth. Only minutes before Tisya leave the family.

Few people stop by around six o'clock. Those who have not been able to come have until the last prayers to do so. There will be a vigil every night until the last prayer, on the seventh day. Tisya is saying the last few words, a short private conversation with every one, privately. She cannot stay away too long. She must return home. Home for her is another country called United States!

- Our old lady is gone, says Anayiz. Gone forever. She left discreetly without fanfare. She said goodbye to the world and a fined drizzle starts falling from the heavens.

- *Chut*! Ana, says Tisya. Don't say one more word. Silence means all.

Tisya leans one more time on the lounge chair her mother used to lay on, looking at the mountains before her eyes. She is ready to go back to Port-au-Prince. She hears a voice calling her from the foot of the mountain. It's Madan Sovè...

-Tisya! Tisya! Where are you?

It had been so long since anybody had called her Tisya.

Tika feels as if she is in a dream. She was just recently on a cruise and now she is in the countryside in Dèyè Lagon. Life is like a rubber band! She thinks about Steve going to Harvard, going to live with students from the American upper class. She sighs.

Waiting for the chauffeur of the rented Jeep, Tika lays on a hay mat on the front porch of her mother's house, taking a last breath of air before leaving. She does not know whether she will ever come back. Her niece, Asefi, who has never gone to school, is massaging her feet. Her nephew Tinason is fanning her to keep flies away and create some breeze..

Everyone took care of her. Everyone gave her warm attention. For her family here, she is somebody important. She is the only one who went to school in the capital. The only one who married a *big shot* from Bois Verna, in Port-au-Prince. She is the only one with a high school diploma. Top on that, her children are Americans. She is probably an American citizen too...

Tika is the only one in her family who left Dèyè Lagon. She is the head of her family.

And that the life that has chosen her!

The chauffeur arrives. Tika is finally ready to leave. She is returning to Port-au-Prince and take off to Miami this afternoon.

# CHAPTER 15

## The Final One

Tika has been back in Miami for a week. She still does not feel like herself because Steve left home while she was in Haiti. She was not home to see her only son go off to Harvard to start his college life. Tika is sad. Saint Jude, papa! How come you allow that to happen?

However, Steve is special. He has left a letter for his Mom. Tika has read it twelve times already:

*Dear Mom,*

*I never thought you would not be here today because you have always been there to make things happen. I never thought I would be packing without you. I understand the circumstances and I realize too that I am a man now and that it's my turn to make things happen, for me and hopefully, for you too.*

*I want to say before leaving that you are the most wonderful mother in the world. You have made my life, our family life, very special. I am proud of you. I am also proud of being born from Haitian parents. I feel special to be Haitian American. It is you that has given me this pride. I believe I know who my parents are and I have great admiration for both of you.*

*I am proud to be Steve Bonplaisir and I am leaving for Harvard with the immense pride that I have inherited from your sense of dignity and your simplicity. I know what your expectations are, I also know what my father is expecting from me. Do not worry, my expectations are the same as yours: I am leaving to succeed and I will succeed.*

*I wanted you to be here today, Mother. I would have kissed you god bye with all my love. I would have told you how much I love you. I know if you were here, you would have done all my packing but Dad and I packed and it was cool to spend this moment with him. In a way that's fine because I had to take responsibility for myself. I am ready for that. You prepared me for that.*

*I am leaving now, it's time to go to the airport. I love you. Leave my room as it is, don't put anything away. I'll be back in three months.*

*Love you dearly,*

*Steve*

If you want to read more about the Bonplezi Family, we recommend you to read *Sezisman*!, another novel also published by Educa Vision and written by Maude Heurtelou. The English title is *Reversals*.

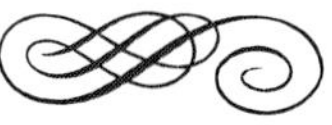

## *What People have said about the Bonplezi Family:*

This is the most powerful and realistic Haitian novel I have ever reviewed. The atmosphere is created masterfully and the reader becomes a participating witness in the tragedies and the excitements of the Bonplezi family. You will not want to miss a second of it.

*Allan Reese*

This is the first time a book speaks of Haitians so well. I see myself in the book, I recognize people I know among the characters. I like Maude's style, it keeps my interest up until the last page. Something unexpected is always happening. You will have a good time reading the book. You will feel like reading it over and over again.

*Wowo Bontan*

It's a lively novel. It has renewed my ties with Haiti and the Haitians.

*Pat Larson*

Ever since Maude has been talking to me about her project of writing the *Bonplezi Family*, I became excited about it, because I knew it was going to be a valuable contribution. In this book, you find different Haitians. The book talks about

Haitians in the United States and Haitians in Haiti. Once you start reading it, you won't be able to put it down.

*Edouard Jean-Pierre*

John D. Nickrosz, as a translator acts as a go-between to reveal to us the literature of other cultures and languages, knowing that quite a lot from the source can never be carried over efficiently in another language. His translation of *Lafami Bonplezi* is an achievement, because he preserves the simplicity and poignancy of the scenes, keeps the forceful Creole narrative drive as well as nuances, and overtones. John made it a must to preserve the originality of the book. This is a great accomplishment.

*Féquière Vilsaint*

… It feel like I really know *The Family Bonplezi*. There is a universality to the immigrant experience… I could see many of my older relatives when I was a child… In fact, there was never a time in my youth that we did not have a least one relative living with us. Maude's poetry is quite powerful…"

*Dan Connolly*

This is a book that speaks well of Haitians. I see myself in it. I recognize people I know too. I like Maude's style, it keeps my interest up until the last page. Something unexpected is always happening. I have a wonderful time reading the book. The readers will feel like reading it over and over again.

*Wowo Bontan*